Ron Collins is one of our best hard science fiction writers—a novel from him is a major event. Enjoy!

Robert J. Sawyer
Hugo Award–winning author of *Quantum Night*

STARFLIGHT

STEALING THE SUN: BOOK 1

RON COLLINS

SKYFOX
PUBLISHING
Science Fiction

STARFLIGHT

STEALING THE SUN: BOOK 1

Cover Images:
© Aleksandar Mirkovic | Dreamstime.com – Sun Over Planet
© Algol | Dreamstime.com - Spaceship With Blue Engine Glow Photo

Skyfox Publishing

ISBN: 1-946176-00-1
ISBN-13: 978-1-946176-00-4

STEALING THE SUN

includes

STARFLIGHT

STARBURST

STARFALL

STARCLASH

STARBORN

Other Work by Ron Collins

Saga of the God-Touched Mage
includes

Glamour of the God-Touched
Target of the Orders
Trail of the Torean
Gathering of the God-Touched
Pawn of the Planewalker
Changing of the Guard
Lord of the Freeborn
Lords of Existence

Picasso's Cat & Other Stories

Five Magics

Six Days in May

Follow Ron at:
http://www.typosphere.com
Twitter: @roncollins13

For Dennis, who would have loved it.

Absence of evidence is not evidence of absence.

Carl Sagan

CONTENTS

INTRODUCTION

This entire series grew out of a short story I wrote during a stint at the Writers of the Future Workshop. I guess you could say it's had quite the birthing process.

That short story was originally titled "Stealing the Sun"—sound familiar?—and was picked up the first place I sent it, which happened to be *Analog*, edited by Stan Schmidt. Dr. Schmidt added a coda to his acceptance letter—basically asking to see what happens next.

This was cool because, you see, I hadn't really thought about that. But we chatted about a few things, and ideas popped and out came "The Taranth Stone," which I was terribly pleased with because (1) I loved it, (2) it got me an original Kelly Freas cover…which is cooler than cool, and (3) some folks at CompuServe decided they liked it well enough to give it one of their HOMer awards. Of course, a third short story, "Parchment in Glass," followed, after which Stan said, "Okay, now go write the novel."

Which I proceeded to do.

And do again.

And, working with agents and other folks, do yet again.

But it wasn't working, you know?

I kept coming back to this story for years, constantly trying to cram it together. The short stories all work. Just tweak this or rethink that, and the novel will be good, right? But every time I plugged it in, it just didn't feel right.

Two years ago, when I had just finished publishing *The Saga of The God-Touched Mage* and I was thinking about what my next project should be, I looked at Stealing the Sun and got that itch again. The story would sneak into my brain in the quiet moments, and my fingers would long for the keyboard.

But this time was different. Because I had just come off a series, I was finally thinking along the idea of plotting more complex stories, and finally—after all these cycles—I understood how these short stories were supposed to go together.

This thing isn't a book, it's a series!

Holy cows! That's it!

I would like to say that at this point, the entire thing just fell together, but that would be a lie. Yes, it all kind of worked, but while piecing the series together I realized why things weren't working when I tried to make this into one book.

The five books that now comprise *Stealing the Sun* tell a story that sprawls across a bunch of light years and, despite being set in a world that is discovering faster-than-light travel, gives a reasonable glance at the relativistic nature of space travel. Space is a pretty big place, of course, and when you tell a space-based story set in a "realistic" setting—whatever "realistic" means when you're talking two hundred years out, anyway—a lot of things happen on their own. And they take time. And time moves as time moves.

I found I had to replot the plot, so to speak.

Figure out precisely what went where.

So, in the end it went like this …

The original short story shows up in book 1, pretty much as you might expect, with only limited changes.

Fans of "The Taranth Stone" are going to have to wait until book 3 to get a real glimpse into its depths.

And that third story?

Well, the events told in those pages are now spread across the books in ways that wouldn't have worked in the past when I was trying to cram it all into a single place.

So, yeah.

It's been a strange process putting this one together, but it's been worth it.

I really love this piece…er…these five pieces.
I hope you do, too.

Ron Collins
August 2016

CHAPTER 1

Alpha Centauri A was chosen for a few very simple reasons. First, it was close, a mere 4.3 light-years from Earth. Second, it was a G2-type star similar enough to the sun that data taken directly from Sol could be used in software models without complex conversions.

The most important factor, though, was greed.

Each star in the Alpha Centauri system had adequate fusion material to support the new Star Drive propulsion systems, but Centauri A was the largest of the three, with a mass ten times that of Proxima and 20 percent greater than Centauri B. The supply of resources in A would last that much longer.

In the end, this was the factor that doomed the star to an accelerated death.

Launch

Chapter 2

UGIS *Everguard*
Ship Local Date: May 5, 2204
Ship Local Time: 1425

Lieutenant Commander Torrance Black stood on the gunmetal runway that circled *Everguard*'s pod engineering assembly area. The rail was cold against his grip. Machinery ozone seeped through the deck's grate and hung in the open space like acrid memories, unchangeable and vaguely distant.

Everything appeared to be on plan.

Each tube bay stood open, the collection forming a perfectly spaced row of a dozen chambers, their three-meter spans empty, pristinely round, and gleaming with stainless steel beauty. The wormhole pods that went into these tubes were the size of G-class riders—thirty meters tip to tip with rounded cross sections that fit into circular launch tubes. Rugged brown thermal material gave them a stark, utilitarian appearance in the brightly lit assembly area. Each end of the pods was capped with conical black boots of heat-treated alloy, banded with a titanium-steel composite fashioned in the zero-g environment of Aldrin Station.

His staff wore fresh whites. Their voices echoed with professional bearing in the open expanse. A computer reported the status of the automated routine controlling the launch sequence.

"I want these tubes loaded by 1800 hours, folks," he barked

with what even he realized was too much vinegar.

"We'll make it, LC," Malloy replied with a quick salute.

Torrance returned the gesture halfheartedly, then stepped into his glass-enclosed office. Malloy was the chief operations officer on this assignment, and trustworthy enough to keep things on track by himself. Torrance settled into his chair, sighed, and stared through a holographic image of the wormhole pod's internal guts.

LC.

Lieutenant commander.

The title echoed in his mind.

That was the thing about rank in the military.

Everyone understood what it meant. Rank labeled a man. It stayed with him. It would not be long before the promotion list was made public—not long before everyone knew where Torrance stood.

He would change the world today. As chief launch engineer, he would release a dozen wormhole pods that would burrow into Alpha Centauri A. Their external shells would burn away inside the star's core, and if at least nine of the twelve systems made it to the target point, they would rend space and create the far end of a wormhole. Raw hydrogen and helium would flow to the other side, where fellow crew members would latch these extradimensional warps to the back end of starships.

Then the universe would be open for the first time.

Faster-than-light travel.

Sirius for breakfast, the Aldebaran double star for dinner.

It would change everything, even the name of the command he worked for. From the moment the pods took hold, Solar Command, the United Government's chief projection of force, would be reborn as Interstellar Command. *Everguard*—complete with 2,158 crew members and their families, and a soon-to-be obsolete propulsion system—was the first cruiser to carry the United Government *Interstellar* Ship (UGIS) designation, but it would not be the last.

He supposed he should feel something appropriate.

But Kip Levitt, the ship's propulsion officer, and a man Torrance had gone to school with so many years ago, had been promoted to full commander today.

Torrance had not.

And it didn't take a lifer to know that when a person in the chain of command is passed over for promotion, their career, for all effective purposes, is over.

"You have a call from Ensign Yarrow," Abke said. The comm light flashed on his desktop.

"Pass it through," he replied.

ABKE was an acronym for Autonomic Bioprocessing Knowledge Engine, the quantum-linked, microbiotic processing intelligence that operated the United Government's solar-system-wide network. Like every other system aboard *Everguard,* this mission represented its first test as an interstellar device. Not surprisingly, it had passed with full colors. Quantum entanglement was his generation's relativity, tested at every turn, passing every test.

An ensign's face filled his primary view screen. "All the tubes are loaded, sir. Power system is charged, and final prognostics are running."

"Thank you," Torrance replied. "We are on hold until the admiral arrives."

"Aye, sir, I'll tell Lieutenant Malloy."

The display changed back to the software circuitry Torrance had been working with before the call. He pressed a control pad to access the propulsion system. Green numbers read three-hundred-plus terra electron volts. A collider ringed the ship at a radius of five kilometers. Outside the observation panel, light from Centauri A made the ring gleam like a silver slash against the velvet blackness of space.

Torrance grimaced with something akin to jealousy.

The particles inside the ring were lucky. Their fate was revealed on a time scale of picoseconds.

He sighed.

Every member of the pod team had filled other jobs during the first leg of the journey, and would be reassigned to them during the trip home. Lieutenant Karl Malloy—his chief operations officer, for example—was a navigation system support specialist, second class, a job that amounted to gathering and processing data from the shipboard controllers to make sure they were still working. When Torrance wasn't launching probes he was the chief service engineer responsible for resolving problems with anything from fried communications systems to stopped-up toilets.

Not exactly glamorous.

But then, that could be said about his entire career.

He had never been one to seek limelight—not like Levitt, anyway. He hadn't been a zero-grav football hero at the academy or a leading officer candidate. He didn't grab control in survival school in times of emergency. Instead, Torrance faced difficult times by separating himself, filling his thoughts with code or whatever technical issue happened to raise its head that day. Hell, the entire *Everguard* mission was really just another case of burying his head in the sand.

He rose from his upholstered chair and stepped around the curved surface of his desk to enter the main assembly area. At the same moment, the far doors dilated and Admiral Robert Hatch entered the bay with a full escort of petty officers and assistants, including Torrance's CO, Captain Alexandir Romanov, and Government Security Officer Malcolm Casey.

"Admiral on the floor," Torrance shouted briskly, and presented a stiff-backed salute.

"As you were," the admiral replied.

Hatch was an older man with brown hair that showed gray at the razor line of his nonexistent sideburns. His green eyes sparkled, and he walked with an efficient stride that spoke of attention to detail and purpose of mind. "What is our status, Lieutenant Commander?"

"Green for launch, sir."

"That's very good. Your team is a credit to the service, Torrance."

"Thank you, sir," Torrance replied, glancing toward Captain Romanov.

Romanov smiled. "Indeed they are."

The captain's presence burned against Torrance's mind. *Indeed they are.* What bullshit. Without doubt it had been Romanov, a rigid, by-the-book-at-all-costs leader, who allowed the promotion billet to pass Torrance by.

Torrance held his tongue and, instead, admired the admiral's calm.

This was an important day for Hatch.

Once the pods were launched and the wormholes stabilized, the admiral would accept a position on the United Government's advisory council for the exploration of space. Mess hall rumors said Interstellar Command would use him as a PR lever at a time when it could cost trillions to build a proper Star Drive spacecraft. As such, the first formal Star Drive mission would rendezvous with *Everguard* in only a few days, and Hatch would shuttle off to Earth, leaving Romanov to command the seven-and-a-half-year return flight.

Technically it was possible to shuttle every member of the crew off *Everguard* in such a fashion if the UG wanted to. But it was actually cheaper to pay a crew to return the ship than it was to run the number of Star Drive missions it would take to do the job—and the fact was that *Everguard* would stand as a museum piece, and a symbol. Obsolete or not, no one wanted to cast her adrift.

Torrance gave the final authorization for "Go Launch," and watched his staff work. It helped him take his mind off the idea of Romanov at the helm.

The crew checked each status display, and inspected the firing assemblies, safety releases, and guidance systems. They closed the hatches of each tube, leaving a dozen anodized black disks evenly spaced along the curved wall, an image that made Torrance think of rounds in an old Remington Colt.

Power surged inside the launch system.

Twelve external launch doors dilated open with the recognizable groan of hydraulic pressure.

"Ten seconds to engage," a recorded voice echoed the readout that hung on the wall.

The room fell to an awkward silence.

The electric essence of tension wrapped itself around him, and his spine tingled with the idea that his entire life was tied up in these twelve wormhole pods. Without realizing why, Torrance wondered about his mother and father. With the time it took message traffic to travel from Earth to *Everguard*, it was possible they were no longer even alive.

The digital readout showed 00:07.

Power coils whined as they sucked energy from the collider.

Torrance recalled years at the academy, his first posting under Captain Jao. Torrance had worked through the ranks, receiving solid commendations at every posting. But opportunities for advancement at LC were limited, and Romanov was by-the-book.

Five seconds.

Everguard traveled at nearly six-tenths the speed of light, which including acceleration and braking, translated into what was roughly a fifteen-local-year round-trip. By the time they returned home, the effects of time dilation meant the rest of the world would have aged an additional three years beyond that. Eighteen years, total for them. For the first time in a long while, he thought of Adrienne.

Three seconds.

Software controllers ran on optical processors.

He would be forty-one standard years old when he arrived home.

Two.

His investments would likely have doubled twice—not that there had been much left after the divorce, but it should be enough to get by on for a while. At least that was something.

One.

"Launch initiated, sir."

The compartment held its breath. Silence echoed where there should have been thunder.

"What's wrong?" the admiral asked.

"I have no idea, sir," Torrance replied, his heart growing cold. "But the pods are not away."

Chapter 3

UGIS *Everguard*
Ship Local Date: May 6, 2204
Ship Local Time: 0125

"We're not getting anywhere, sir," the technician said.

"And your point would be?" Torrance snapped back.

The tech just sat there, stammering while nothing came out.

The glass boards flickered with displays of the launch system's microcircuitry and software execution paths.

The air in Pod Engineering was warm and stale, a feeling that reminded Torrance of late nights in the electronics laboratory back in his college days, but not in a good way. He didn't like the omnipresent blanket of maudlin disappointment that pressed over him whenever he looked back to times when the future was still the future, but, like it or not, he had been doing just that all day.

It made him brain-dead.

Everything about today made him brain-dead.

The staff was tired, too. Their mission-day whites hung from their bodies like whipped flags in dead wind. Every nook and corner of the place smelled of day-old sweat.

"I'm sorry," Torrance said. He rubbed cheeks that were plastic with fatigue. "I'm just like you folks, though—really frustrated, and heading toward mad as hell. Romanov wants a personal report at 0600, and I'll admit I don't have a clue about what to tell him. I apologize for snapping, all right?"

The staff all nodded.

Lieutenant Malloy spoke up with a grin. "Maybe Romanov would like to come down and check it out personally. Maybe take a little ride in the tube." His eyebrow raised in mock anticipation, his left hand rose in a flying motion, and he made a whooshing sound. "We could probably arrange a close-up inspection."

The team chuckled, and the room loosened noticeably.

Malloy had a knack for saying the right thing at the right time.

The image of Romanov drifting out into space from a derelict launch tube made everyone smile.

Torrance took a deep breath.

"We've been over everything three times. If the problem was on board, we'd have found it by now."

"What do you mean, LC?"

"Maybe the answer isn't here. Maybe it's something outside."

"Like what?"

Torrance scratched the stubble on his cheek. "I don't know. How about we run the full spectrum of sensor scans again, okay?"

"Did that hours ago, sir," Malloy replied.

Torrance shrugged. "Maybe we missed something."

Malloy nodded. "Okay, LC. We'll do it."

The crew stood to get to work.

"When you finish the scan," Torrance said, "I want everyone to turn in for the night, all right?"

An hour later, Torrance was at External Sensor Command. The scan had completed fifteen minutes ago, and now he was discussing the results with Silvio Nivead, one of the ship's several signal processing specialists.

"You're kidding me, right?" Torrance said.

Nivead looked up at Torrance with his dark eyes ringed in folds of sepia skin, and his balding head gleaming in the lab's bright light. "You know I don't kid about these kinds of things," he replied in a clipped accent that was at least part Portuguese despite having grown up primarily in Lunar province.

Torrance knew no such thing.

Nivead had been with the service since the days of optical processors and multidimensional atomic storage systems. At one point or another he had probably worked on every important galactic surveying team that had been put together in the twenty years prior to *Everguard*'s flight. As bright and experienced as he was, however, there was a reason Nivead was still working second shift—and that reason was an attitude as thick as mayonnaise.

Silvio expected people to think like him, only less quickly. He had no patience when they didn't conform to his frame of mind, and a hair trigger when it came to letting them know about it. He was legendary for making it known he came from an old-school family, multilingual and rigid in their adherence to a doctrine that was equal parts perfection and self-reliance. When you worked with Silvio Nivead you knew two things: the product would be good, and you would not escape unscathed.

So, yes, it was actually *just like* Silvio Nivead to kid about such a thing.

"The pattern is all over the place," Nivead said. "But the signal itself is cohesive at just under seven hundred kilohertz."

"Microwave radio?"

"On the low end, but yessiree, Lieutenant Commander, I can report to you with great certainty that these are most definitely radio wavelengths."

Torrance absorbed Silvio's sarcasm without comment.

"Where's it coming from?" Torrance asked.

"Got me, boss-man."

"Would that signal be enough to interfere with the launch?"

"They could pitch a bit of crosstalk if the traces get close enough." Silvio pursed his thick lips, the bottom one protruding in a way that reminded Torrance of his grandfather. "It would take a lucky strike, but odder things have happened. Science is like that, you know, LC?"

"Yes," Torrance snapped. "I know a little about science."

Nivead looked like a cat in sunshine, and Torrance was immediately mad at himself.

He ran his hand through close-cropped hair, then down along the roughness of his chin. All business, he thought. That's how you had to deal with guys like Silvio Nivead. He was usually better about keeping Silvio from getting the better of him, but he was so tired now. He should have followed his own orders and hit the rack, but his mind was running loops he couldn't stop.

Given the way the last twenty-four standard hours had gone, it would be just his luck that stray emissions from a randomly emitting interstellar radio source would crap on his launch.

"What could have caused signals like that?" Torrance finally said.

The whites of Silvio's eyes grew wide enough that he looked like a cartoon character. "You're gonna have to tell me, boss-man. I'm just a data hack."

"Has the star been active?" Torrance replied.

Silvio looked like he was going to say something, but instead the tech just punched up the star system's frequency spectrum and let it run on a twenty-four-hour compression.

Yes, Torrance thought.

All business.

Silvio stared at the display as he paged through density images.

The three stars—Centauri A, Centauri B, and Proxima (which the crew had taken to calling the little red dwarf)—collected together to make the boot of the Earth's constellation Centaurus. A, also known as Rigel Kent, was the biggest, and brightest. Torrance stared at the same data Silvio did, noting the readout of the star's power density and rotational speed, 22.62 days. The star was nearing the portion of its orbit that took it farthest away from its closest sibling, Centauri B.

"We've got a little something something going on here," Silvio said, pointing to a holo display of the star. "But its density in the seven hundred K range is flat as a board. Can't see the star had much to do with anything."

"What else is out there?"

Silvio leaned back and laced his hands behind his head. "Gee, I don't know, boss. Standard background radiation from Centauri B. Proxima. The planets. Then there's the fun stuff from deep space. And if we hit the rotor-scan system we'll get all those beautiful pictures from the galaxies."

"Proxima is too far away to worry about."

Silvio's grin faded a nano-lumen.

"Eyeballing that signal strength," he said, "I would bet my left pinky that B's too far away, too."

"Can you run a frequency scan, just to be sure?"

"It's technically possible."

Torrance tilted his head at the analyst to say his official patience was almost gone.

"What?" Silvio said. "You don't trust me?"

"Your word is good as gold, Sil. But Romanov is on my ass right now and I can't afford to miss this."

"Always a bigger fish, eh, LC?" Silvio gave a sage grin.

"Can you run the scan?"

"Your wish is my command, Squanto." He turned to his station and issued the proper commands to carry out Torrance's request.

"Squanto?" Torrance said, hoping his annoyance wasn't showing.

Nivead's grin grew deeper, but he just shrugged.

"Why Squanto?"

"I don't know. It just sounds right on you."

Torrance turned back to his own station.

Oh, to have that kind of courage, he thought. There were advantages to being more like Silvio. Just do your job, do it very well, and let whatever happens flow by like so much river flotsam. He wondered if Silvio had been born this way or if he had just crossed a "don't give a shit" line somewhere along the way of his career.

If so, maybe someday Torrance could cross that line, too.

In the meantime, he needed to look at the radio data coming from the planets.

"Abke," he said, "I need access to data file A-Planet-1."

"File available."

The holographic image of a brown-and-black planet rotated slowly over the desktop. Data defining its mass, density, orbit, and ecliptic tilt displayed beside the image.

It was the innermost of the system's planets, and carried the official handle of Apple, named in the days after the second planet had been dubbed Eden. But while the computer labeled it by that formal title (as well as the usual stream of alphanumeric gibberish the scientific world worked under), everyone aboard knew the rock as Alpha-Alpha, the first planet in the Alpha Centauri A system. It was immediately shortened to "Alfalfa."

All total the Centauri A system included five planets: Alpha, Eden, Gamma, Delta, and Epsilon (which the crew has also dubbed as "Mata Hari," because its orbit was large enough that some thought it was likely to jump ship and become a satellite in the Centauri B system).

"Please map infrared data, Abke," Torrance said.

The image of the surface changed to swirling patterns—orange, white, and yellow on the side closest to the star, cooling to darker shades of blue on the far side. Alfalfa had an eight-hour day and no atmosphere, resulting in a surface that passed thermal radiation straight through to deep space. A jagged blue-and-black network indicated the topography of the planet. It was highly cratered, and at this resolution its deep crevasses and heavily ridged scars were clearly visible, but nothing there seemed relevant to his problem.

"Infrared data is fifty-eight percent actual, forty-two percent derived," Abke said. "Would you like to see raw data only?"

Everguard wasn't in the best position to pick up data from the planet, so Abke was extrapolating.

"No. Give me radar, please. Multiple scans from five hundred to nine hundred kilohertz. Focus on seven hundred. Twenty-four-hour repeating loop."

He scanned the result, but still didn't see anything relevant.

Story of his life, really.

Despite skills that were always solid and respected, nothing seemed to ever quite work out for him. At the end of the day, he had always been just a talented grunt. Which is the message Alfalfa's display seemed to be whispering to him. Nothing here for you, it said. Go back to your basic engineering and leave the important findings to the anointed guys, like Kip Levitt.

He remembered a night with his dad—a man who had always worked hard, but was happy making a simple living that consisted of things like fixing plumbing or installing air quality systems in Mrs. Krespah's ventilation ducts. Torrance was a third-year student on that night, and was studying the differential calculus needed to understand the lab simulations of planetary origins, but things hadn't been working out right. It was late, like it was now, and Torrance was feeling drained and quite a bit less than competent.

"You don't got to work like that," his dad had said. "They won't let you win, anyway."

"It's not like that," Torrance had replied.

His dad had shrugged.

Torrance remembered every nuance of that shrug now.

It would have been fine if he had just left it there, but his dad never was the kind to leave such a thing lay, and he was a man who had even less patience for theorists than he did for managers.

"You're no Einstein, you know?" he said in his sleepy Midwestern tone.

The phrase, and all that it carried, echoed in Torrance's mind as he looked at the readout. You're no Einstein. Of course he wasn't. But, there had to be something more to him than this. There should be more to life than fixing toilets and replacing sound systems, and…

And, you know, guys like Kip Levitt aren't exactly Albert Einstein, either.

He cleared his head.

He had work to do, and the fact that he was letting the memory of his father and the aura of Kip Levitt keep him from doing it just pissed him off that much more.

"Let's do the same for file A-Planet-2, please."

The projection flickered, and a model of Eden replaced Alfalfa.

It was larger than the first planet.

Eden was nearly the size of Earth, with a five-degree tilt and a weak magnetic field offset seven degrees from its polar rotation. The image provided was in the optical spectrum, hence showed nothing beyond the striated but gauzy ball of orange-yellow haze that was the planet's sulfuric ionosphere.

"Infrared, please, Abke."

The planet turned a pinkish orange, almost uniform in aspect, bleeding to purple at the outer edge of its circumference. Eden was similar to Venus in that its dense cloud cover served to distribute heat globally, resulting in a temperature that probably didn't vary by more than a few degrees between night and day or even up through its atmospheric altitude.

Right now the graph showed 52.7 degrees on the Celsius scale, 127 degrees Fahrenheit. Quite balmy.

"Radar, please. Same parameters as with A-1."

The image changed to reveal the lower hemisphere as a cracked and crevassed wasteland, not as cratered as Apple, presumably because the dense atmosphere ate up smaller meteors that would normally have impacted the surface otherwise. In an odd way the digitized landscape reminded Torrance of his training camp on Europa—Eden's surface could be the hellish twin to Europa's icy badlands. Eden's northern hemisphere was also desolate, but scarred with a massive ring of raised ridges tall enough to register green on the topographical image.

The entire surface was covered in flows that told the geologists that the surface had been constantly reconfiguring itself as a result of the planet's volcanism and rapid geological activity. He tried to gauge the size of one massive area of the roughed-up land. It was maybe the size of Olympus Mons—say six hundred kilometers across—and the fact that this feature was so prominent in the light of the rest of the planet's relatively flat surface suggested to some that it had been created by a single huge impact that threw material into the atmosphere and dumped it there as if it was one big shovelful.

The idea made Torrance grin. He loved those kinds of analogies. They were silly, but powerful enough that he could create the image of Hercules or some kind of Greek god with a shovel bent over the planet.

Suddenly a white flare rose and fell from just outside that raised zone.

Torrance blinked. Had he imagined that?

"Can you back up, please?"

"Beginning now, sir," Abke replied.

A blurry flare flashed again at an edge of the mountainous rim.

"Forward," he said.

The flare came again. It was large—as big as his thumb on the model, which would translate to a hundred kilometers on Eden's surface. Torrance watched further. More flares burst, all originating from roughly the same place.

"I need more detail around those flashes, please, Abke."

"None available."

"Looks like you got a helluva storm there, LC," Nivead said as he guided his chair over to take a closer look.

"Yeah," Torrance replied. The file showed another flash, this time flickering before fading. "Abke, please cut the frequency band to a fifty-kilohertz range centered at seven hundred. Put it on a time loop from hour twelve to hour sixteen."

The image continued its sporadic flaring.

"Man-oh-man," Silvio said. His chair groaned as he lay back. "Reminds me of the big ol' dust busters on Mars. Those things whipped up, and you just dug in and waited. But if you could find a safe place, they could light up the sky and it was like the good Lord hisself was paintin' a picture."

"Uh-huh."

"Don't believe me?"

Torrance pointed to the image. "These flashes are too stationary to be a storm, don't you think?"

Nivead shrugged. "I seen storms sit down for a good while, LC. And Eden's got more than her share of cloud cover."

Torrance pursed his lips, and kept his eyes on the image.

It was a fact that dense clouds could distort this kind of signal, but he felt something deeper here and he had been around long enough that he knew he would hate himself forever if he didn't follow up on this.

"Let it run forward, please, Abke."

The stream of flares continued for some time, then came a single large burst. He waited several more minutes, but it didn't come back.

"Guess it's done raining," Silvio said.

Torrance replayed the sequence.

The flares rose and fell in yellow, white, and orange, beautiful in their own right. It was static, though, its source not moving. It could be a storm, he supposed. But it really wasn't like any storm he had ever seen. It looked more like one of the radio towers he had fiddled with when he was a kid putting together com protocols for larks.

The idea hit him cold.

Scientists had studied the Alpha Centauri system for decades prior to *Everguard*'s launch. They listened for signals and imaged the entire system with deep-space telescopes. They scanned with radio interferometers, looking for the telltale wobble or the flickering dimness that identified planets. It was Mars's Kochi Station that announced the discovery of three planets orbiting A and two circling B. Only the second planet from Centauri A, however, was inside the zone where liquid water—and thereby intelligent life—was possible.

Scientists dubbed the planet Eden.

Closer study, however, soon determined it to be anything but a paradise.

Despite the existence of oxygen and the hint of carbon-based amino acids that some scientists still considered bio-tags for prospective life, the outer shell of the planet's atmosphere was a horrific mixture of methane, carbon dioxide, and sulfuric acid that had combined to create a runaway greenhouse effect similar to that of Venus. Models also suggested that the extreme tidal forces of the Alpha Centauri tri-star system were heating the planet's core, and would make for a volcanic world with stormy weather patterns that continually raged across the surface.

The search for intelligent life, the scientists said, would have to dig deeper into the universe.

But now Torrance wondered.

The atmospheric shell was poisonous, yes, but it was still just a blanket. No one had really looked for what could be happening on the surface or even below it.

Could this signal be from an intelligent source?

"Abke," Torrance said. "Can you run this file through primary and secondary linguistic recognition routines?"

"Process initiated," Abke replied. "Estimated to complete in two minutes."

"Linguistics?" Silvio said. "You think the storm is talking to us?"

Torrance started to reply, then saw Silvio's crazy grin. "Sure, Silvio," he finally said. "I think it's ordering a pizza."

Silvio slapped his thigh and gave a laugh.

"Ordering a pizza. That's a good one, LC."

Torrance turned back to the workstation. It had been a very long day, but even if he hit the rack now, Torrance knew he would never get to sleep.

He cracked his knuckles, waiting for Abke to finish.

CHAPTER 4

UGIS *Everguard*
Ship Local Date: May 6, 2204
Ship Local Time: 0520

The good news was that it wasn't his fault.

Torrance stood outside his CO's quarters and gathered his thoughts. He was early, but he didn't figure that would be a problem.

"Romanov here." The captain's voice was alert and responsive through the intercom.

"Lieutenant Commander Black, sir."

The door buzzed, then dilated open.

The ventilation system blew a cool breeze. The room was quiet and calm despite being decorated with a row of flat-panel images of starships and other vehicles. Romanov was fourth-generation military, and the regimentation of his compartment showed it. The far wall, however, carried a holo of a waterfall from the backlands of Maui. A glass table with three chairs sat in the corner. Torrance could almost smell fresh water and island breeze.

The captain rose from his meditation pad, dressed in a loose robe of red terry cloth. A thin film of sweat glistened from the curve of his collarbone.

"Good morning, Captain," Torrance said.

"I think it is acceptable to be informal before 0600, Torrance,"

Romanov said with only a trace of his Russian heritage lingering in his accent. He gestured toward the table. "You look as if you've had a very long night. Have a seat and tell me about it."

Torrance sat down, not certain where to start.

The captain sat across from him.

"We have a problem," Torrance said.

"Yes?"

"When *Everguard* opened the launch doors, we encountered an electromagnetic disturbance."

"I see no problem, then. Shield what we need to shield and get on with it."

"It's not that simple."

"Why not? We have inventory."

"Yes, we do," Torrance admitted. "But the disturbance is coming from outside."

"Outside of what?"

"Outside of *Everguard*, sir. It's coming from the star's second planet."

Romanov's face betrayed nothing as he thought through the ramifications of what Torrance was saying. "Why didn't it show up in our scan?"

"It was there. I checked the logs myself. But the configuration of the planets and the star itself cut the amplitude of what we received. For whatever reason, we overlooked it."

Torrance didn't need to add that the *we* who *overlooked it* did not include either Torrance Black or Alexandir Romanov.

"I see." The captain clasped his hands together and leaned back. "So, am I to assume you're thinking that this stray burst of EMI suggests there may be life on Eden?"

"I don't see how we can read it any other way."

"Despite the fact that all other examinations confirm the planet's atmosphere is toxic?"

"Only a life-form could produce this EMI."

"The planet is a perpetual storm," Romanov said. "It is certainly possible that such a place could generate high-energy disturbances, is it not?"

"What we've received has been tight, Captain, not random white noise."

"Have you run our translator programs?"

"Yes."

"And?"

"Nothing yet, sir. But just because we don't recognize a pattern doesn't mean one can't exist. Our linguistic code should be reviewed before we go any further."

The ventilation system wheezed like the collected mumble of distant voices.

"Lieutenant Commander." The captain's voice became firm, and Torrance realized that, pre-0600 or not, the discussion had just become formal. "We have a mission to accomplish. What you have found is not enough to warrant the conclusion of intelligent life when everything else we know to be true about this planet discounts that."

Torrance froze. He had expected Romanov to point the finger of blame at External Sensor Command and postpone the mission. But now the captain seemed more determined than ever to push forward.

"But what if I'm right, Captain?"

"I don't think that is the case."

"But, sir, if this *is* intelligent life, draining their star will leave them without energy. Whatever civilization exists will die."

"I understand, Torrance," the captain said, his eyes blazing like dark lasers. "But even a simple trip planetside could cost us months both ways. And some very steep odds say all we would find are clouds that generate tight bursts of static. Do you want to be the one who tells the admiral that we're going to hold back our understanding of the entire universe for half a standard year while we piddle around looking for thunderstorms in Eden?"

Torrance did not reply.

"You're a good man, Lieutenant Commander," Romanov continued. "You've always been part of the team. You're a hard worker, and when the going gets tough, you stick your nose into the guts of problems and figure out how to make things work. It is a trait I most admire in you. I know I can rely on you to do what is right for us in the big picture."

Suddenly, Torrance understood.

This was about position. It was about expectations and power.

If *Everguard* diverted for a false call, the careers of every officer aboard would hang in tenuous balance, not the least of which was Alexandir Romanov's.

Now Romanov was staring at him with that firm but fatherly expression that said he expected Torrance to do his part, to play the game as it needed to be played. His CO expected Torrance to go along with him. Go along to get along, his father had once said, and that phrase had buried itself into Torrance's psyche even back then. He had always gone along, but not because he thought it was right or wrong. He had simply ducked his head and gotten work done mostly because he trusted the system—he believed it when everyone said that what really mattered was doing the work. Do the work better than anyone else, and you'll win, they said. Go along to get ahead.

Torrance's eyes slid away from the pressure of Romanov's gaze.

He looked down at his hands. His stomach burned, reminding him that the last thing he had eaten was the synthesized roast beef sandwich he had for lunch yesterday.

"Thank you, sir," Torrance said, more because it seemed he should than because he felt anything.

"I understand your concerns," the captain said. "I'll take your report to the admiral for his confirmation of my order. But our mission is clear. I have a duty to the people of our Solar System, as do you. Those tubes need to be shielded and another launch profile prepared as soon as possible."

"I understand," Torrance said, standing.

"Do you?"

He understood, yes.

He was to be a good soldier and do as he was told. That much was clear. He was to engage in no more discussion of life on Eden. But a cold stone formed in his stomach then because he also understood the captain had just supported potential genocide of what might be an intelligent species, and he had done so with barely a second thought.

"Yes, sir. I do understand."

Romanov nodded.

"Thank you for your work, Lieutenant Commander. I'm sure it has been a busy evening."

Torrance sighed. "I've ordered the staff to their beds, but I think we can be ready to launch in under twenty-four hours."

"Very good. Looks like you could use some sleep yourself."

"Yes, sir," he replied, saluting.

Torrance turned and strode out of the captain's office, his temples suddenly throbbing with a massive headache.

Chapter 5

UGIS *Everguard*
Ship Local Date: May 7, 2204
Ship Local Time: 0830

Torrance stood alone on the officers' radiation-shielded observation deck, and stared into the blackness of space. He had retired early the previous day and, after a fitful rest, woke even earlier this morning. Breakfast had been alone in the main mess. Now he stood with his hands clasped behind his back, thinking deeply about Adrienne for the first time in a very long time.

They had met right after he entered the Academy.

He remembered their wedding day, the sugary whiteness of their cake, and how Adrienne shoved an overly large bite into his mouth. It had been such an exciting day, the beginning of something that seemed so infinite. Adrienne was special—intriguing, and with interesting takes on everything from the politics of the moon to how to best grow lemons in zero gravity. Her Mediterranean background made her fiery at times, which fit against his own Midwestern stoicism in interesting ways. They had wanted children—Adrienne pushing for two, Torrance thinking more like three. But children never came. A series of trips to fertility doctors eventually found he was the problem.

There were solutions, of course: adoption, or donor transplants, gene therapy or clone cultures. But Torrance was adamant that he couldn't raise someone else's children. He didn't care that everyone else was doing it. It didn't feel right, and no gene therapy in the world could change the fact that every time he looked into the child's eyes he would see his own failure.

Yes, it was selfish and stupid.

He could see that now.

But he had been scared and embarrassed, and, as usual, he hid from the problem rather than face it. This was his way when he felt out of control and things got too heavy for him to deal with. He had ignored the problem with Adrienne, and as usual, it had festered.

They split a few months before the *Everguard* opportunity arose.

He had needed something to focus on, something to take the pain away. All he had at hand was the military—with its rules that dictated what to do when and how to do it. It suited him. He felt comfortable here. He understood how it worked. The military had been his life.

The idea of fifteen years aboard *Everguard* had seemed so perfect back then.

Torrance jumped at his pager's piercing bleat.

"You have a call from Lieutenant Malloy, sir," Abke said.

"Pass it through."

"Connection made."

"What can I do for you, Karl?"

"All our sensitive components have been shielded, sir. Do you want us to begin prelaunch preparations?"

"Is the testing done?"

"Yes, sir. No anomalies."

"Yes, then. Prelaunch would be the next step."

"Aye, sir."

Torrance pressed his lips together. The shielding was in place. In something under two hours he would give an order that, knock on wood, *should* open the entire universe to the human species, arguably saving it when looked at over the span of millennia, but might doom another.

There was life on the second planet in the Alpha Centauri A system.

He had no proof of this fact, of course, but he felt it lying there inside the data like it was this invisible fire burning under his skin. He was right. He had to be. Proof or no proof—he felt it.

Something, or some*one*, was there.

No argument the captain or anyone else aboard this ship could put forward would convince Torrance otherwise.

His uniform collar seemed tight against his neck.

His stomach rolled over.

He never asked for this.

His career was likely over. He would return to his own world tired and used up—a man with no family, no future, and no dignity. And now he would return also as a man who felt genocide so deeply in his bones that he thought he might get sick right here on the observation deck.

The thought twisted like a hunting knife in his gut.

He felt powerless, beaten down.

The idea of launching the pods made him feel dirty.

He was one man in the entire existence of the universe.

He had twelve buttons to push.

The numbers, twelve and one, waded through his mind.

He was one lieutenant commander with twelve wormhole pods, there was one star outside this one spaceship that he existed in, and one people with unknown technology on the one planet than existed in that one star's habitable zone.

Unknown technology, yes, but technology at least advanced enough to release emissions that interfered with *Everguard*'s systems.

And he had twelve buttons to push.

An idea dawned.

A thought. A concept, a harebrained idea, perhaps even an audacious brain blunder that gnawed at his belly and made his breathing rise with a sudden change of pattern that let him know he was on to something.

One technology.

A flare of energy burned at his spine.

It could work, he realized.

Competitive reengineering had fueled human progress for centuries. If the aliens he was envisioning were sharp enough, they could figure it out. And if he was right, the intelligence on that planet was at least advanced enough to broadcast radio.

It was a huge personal risk.

His activity would almost certainly show up if Romanov requested another shipwide scan. What was left of his career was certainly at stake.

He gazed out the observation panel and recalled the expression on Romanov's face as Torrance had reported his findings.

The collider glimmered against black velvet.

Protons and neutrons raced inside that ring, scattering themselves into the netherworld of quarks and leptons—universes that lived and died in fractions of seconds. A collector gathered each of these particles, separating them and funneling each into channels where supercooled electromagnets ensured they would find their antimatter counterparts. The resulting meeting of matter and antimatter pushed energy into the ship's propulsion unit. Soon a small fraction of that power would be siphoned to feed the launch tubes.

Torrance closed his eyes, and listened to the gentle hiss of the ship's operational systems. It was a soft sound, warm. It reminded him of the wind that had blown past his open window when he was a teenager in Wisconsin.

That was a long time ago.

Lives, like military careers, can be made in the span of a single collision of a neutron and a proton. They can be broken in similar moments of time. Or they can merely fade away, decaying like radioactive waste with the half-life of a human being.

It was time, Torrance realized, feeling truly comfortable for the first time since he could remember.

He knew what he had to do.

CHAPTER 6

UGIS *Everguard*
Ship Local Date: May 7, 2204
Ship Local Time: 1200

The staff wore their workday blues this time.

"Fifteen seconds until launch," the mission controller said.

Again the admiral stood at Torrance's side, Security Officer Casey and Captain Romanov on the side opposite the admiral. The power coil moaned while switches clicked and firing systems armed.

The countdown clock read 00:10.

Twelve probes stood ready to forge the link that would give the human race the ability to explore millions of stars.

00:05.

Torrance clasped his hands behind him and took in a slow, deep breath.

He felt oddly proud.

He had done his best, and that was all that any God—or any commander, for that matter—had the right to ask of a man. Perhaps it wouldn't be enough, but perhaps it would. And *that* was sometimes the most that any man could ask of himself.

00:02.

00:01.

"Launch sequence initiated," the controller said.

The pods thrust against *Everguard*'s hull like strikes from twelve sledgehammers. A dozen flaming arrows sliced through black space in three formations of four birds apiece.

One group fell toward the star, then another.

Then the last.

A single pod of the final group, however, deviated from the original flight plan.

Adrenaline leapt through Torrance's body. He stifled a proud smile.

His calculations had been rapidly done, the reprogramming equally hasty. But he knew this code like the back of his hand. If he got it right, the pod would land somewhere on the second planet. With luck, whoever was there would examine its circuitry and its propulsion system. With their new knowledge they might learn how to engineer space-faring vessels themselves.

And they might find a way to save themselves.

"What's wrong with that one?" the admiral said.

"I'm not certain, sir," Torrance replied before Captain Romanov could. "But I'll run a full investigation. The good news is that we have eleven birds on course and heading for home. We need only nine to be successful."

Of the remaining pods, one lost power and was pulled to a fiery death in Centauri A's gravity well. The rest pierced the star's surface. Thermal shielding held back the heat for the milliseconds each electronic package needed.

The wormhole actuators engaged.

Energy flowed, hydrogen fusing to helium.

Aboard *Everguard,* Torrance was surrounded by crewmates, all cheering, all wearing shit-eating grins, and all pounding him on the back.

Captain Romanov gave Torrance a guarded glance, but did not say anything.

Celebrations & Preparations

NEWS

SOURCE: INFOWAVE -- NEWS for the twenty-third century
RECEIVED: UGIS EVERGUARD TRANSMITTED VIA UGIS SUNCHASER
TRANS DATE: May 23, 2205, Earth Standard
HEADLINE: Mubadid Confirmed Supreme President

In an emergency session, the combined Earth country-states and Solar System sub-governments passed a bill today that provides Executive President Laney Mubadid formal governance of the home galaxy.

"This is an important day for all human beings," Mubadid said as she accepted the additional responsibility. "Expansion and exploration has always been the way of humanity. From the days of our first ancestors in the Olduvai Gorge to the Roman Empire and Magellan's travels, from the Louisiana Purchase to the earliest climbers of Everest, humanity has always striven to see the unseen and know the unknown. This is how we ensure our survival.

"Today we have a unified government that will ensure we proceed in a bold manner, and a manner that will preserve the dignity of our entire galaxy of star systems."

Chapter 7

UGIS *Everguard*
Ship Local Date: May 16, 2204
Ship Local Time: 0750

Numbers glowed from the glass desktop in Alexandir Romanov's office. A mug of green tea, half-empty, sat at the edge of the table. He rubbed his temple and moved 250,000,000 solar dollars from the budget line for refitting the fitness center, and split it in three directions—150,000,000 to optimize electromagnets in the collider system, 75,000,000 to repair Central Deck's main corridor, and 25,000,000 to refurbish the core of the power grid that continued to show signs of deterioration.

Romanov looked at the numbers and couldn't help but grimace. Creating a budget was just what he wanted to be doing the day after the admiral's party.

What a waste of time.

Somewhere someone in the UG structure had gotten the idea that costs could be lowered if each ship had to vie for budget each year, that somehow their competitive natures would cause each commander to reduce expenditures in a quest to run the tightest ship. It would never work, of course. Whoever had that idea didn't understand the territorial law of one-upmanship among the elite of the Admiralty, the best of which would simply prey upon the few who actually did reduce cost by grabbing the suddenly excess budget.

So, as each top admiral wrested larger and larger slices of the pie the administrators—in turn—would placate the rest by increasing the size of the pie. Costs would ratchet, and the bean-counters would scratch their heads and go back to the drawing board to try to figure out what went wrong.

To make matters even sillier, the time gap between interstellar flight and time dilation of sub-light-speed travel made the idea more outdated than an abacus. He would love to be an invisible spider on the wall at the budget briefings with the Commerce Commission's chronal consultant—a position whose single duty was to synchronize budget calls to each space-faring ship and ensure their input was properly factored.

The image of a bureaucrat doing relativistic math while balancing a budget brought him a delicious sense of smugness. Romanov was a military man from a family of military men. He understood and appreciated the sense of comedic timing one needed to survive bureaucracy.

He moved the 250,000,000 solar dollars back to the fitness center.

What were they going to do—radio him four years ago to tell him he couldn't fix the power grid?

His calendar today was back-to-back meetings, including a session with Lieutenant Commander Black in a few minutes, lunch with the admiral to discuss transfer of command, and a late session with Security Officer Casey that would be his opportunity to give his official update on intelligence progress related to the launch failure.

He didn't like Casey.

The man hit every stereotype you could gin up about security officers. He was prissy and closed-minded. He dressed in his formals most of the time, and held himself like he'd been spun up a half-turn too far. He liked wine with his dinner, but never more than one glass and often even just half that. Romanov once had Casey as a teammate during a training exercise, and all the man did the entire session was question whether material that supported the program was being managed properly.

He sighed.

The idea of spending an hour answering Casey's questions was as appealing as scrubbing himself down with a field of thistle, but once Romanov took command Casey was going to be his government anchor (as every captain of every UGIS ship in existence called them), and nothing was more dangerous to a career than having a disgruntled anchor aboard a long-haul ship. Best get used to it, and best get a feel for how to deal with him now.

He looked at his slate again.

Dinner with leadership command was scheduled for 1900.

Somewhere in there, he wanted to stop at Propulsion Command to see how his son was doing. He hadn't talked to Andre in over a week.

He sipped his tepid tea, and ran his tongue around his mouth to get rid of the grainy aftertaste. The mug was decorated with green swirls that reminded Romanov of leaves.

He missed leaves.

They were, perhaps, the most perfect of all creations—fragile and beautiful, but resilient at the same time. Coarse and aromatic, dense and green. He thought of Lani with her brown eyes waiting for him in Oahu. He remembered the blue waves in her dress at the landing, her soft hands on his face as he kissed her good-bye. She had stayed behind to care for her mother and her father as they aged. It had been a very long time since he had seen her.

"Lieutenant Commander Black to see you, sir," Abke said, breaking his reverie.

He drew his hand back from the mug.

"Let him in," he said.

The door slid back.

"You wanted to see me, sir?" Torrance said as he entered.

Romanov gestured toward an empty chair. Torrance settled into place.

"That was a gutsy move, Torrance."

"I beg your pardon?"

"I've examined the preflight records. The last probe's navigation software was altered."

Torrance considered denying it, but could see the firmness in his CO's eyes. "They deserved a chance, sir."

The captain nodded. "Did you know I have a meeting with

Security Officer Casey later this afternoon?"

"No, sir. I don't have access to your calendar."

"He wants to review the failed launch."

"I see."

"I am certain he will also want to speak with you, Lieutenant Commander. Standard protocol on such an event, I'm afraid."

Torrance took a deep breath before he could control himself. Romanov was right. It made sense that the Government Security Officer would speak with him, but it hadn't been something Torrance had considered until now. The idea put a knot in his stomach.

"I assume you are aware that deliberately altering a mission profile without authorization can get a man court-martialed."

Silence reigned for several heartbeats, during which Torrance contemplated such appetizing things as lifelong exiles. Romanov's gaze felt as heavy as a lead blanket in an X-ray chamber.

"We're stealing their sun, sir," Torrance finally said. "I figure they've got maybe ten thousand years before their planet gets too cold to support life. If they're of advanced technology, maybe they'll be able to study the pod and save themselves."

"And if they're not?"

Torrance stared into the wall scene of the Ural Mountains and waited for the captain to speak. He wondered if it would be court-martial, or merely some form of censure. Certainly he would lose at least one rank.

"You don't have a family, do you?" Romanov said.

"My parents live in Wisconsin."

"I mean children."

Torrance furrowed his brow. "No, sir. No children."

Romanov gave an indecipherable grunt and absentmindedly fingered his cup of cold tea. "I'm sorry you were passed over for promotion, Torrance. You are a good man, but we have only so many billets."

"Thank you, sir."

"You've done your part with Eden, now, isn't that right, Lieutenant Commander?"

"Sir?"

"The official cause of the launch failure is logged as a particularly violent storm on Eden. The pod is wherever it is."

"That's correct, sir."

"That means you've done what you could. Assuming there is something to your idea, which there is almost certainly *not*, you've given them a lifeline."

"Yes, sir."

"So we can leave this here, correct?"

"What do you mean?"

Romanov stood up, stepped slowly around his desk, and came to sit on its corner, his arms crossed and a disappointed expression on his lined face. "Torrance," he finally said. "You understand the value of the command structure, correct? You understand that each member of the crew has a function?"

"Yes, sir."

"And you understand that if this ship is to operate smoothly, each function needs to do what it is supposed to do, when it is supposed to do it?"

"Yes, sir."

"And that the design of this structure has been specifically created with the idea that setting the goals of what is acceptable activity and what is not acceptable activity lies entirely in my leadership team?"

The question hung in the air like an empty noose.

"I understand, sir."

"That's good," Romanov said. He uncrossed his arms and rubbed his palms over his thighs, finishing with a sigh. "You've always worked hard, Torrance. It is a long flight back home. A lot of good things can happen to a man who works hard for seven years."

Torrance stared at his CO, as the man returned to his seat.

Romanov regarded him openly.

The depth of his brown gaze told Torrance everything he needed to know.

The captain had made a snap decision about the mission, but he had understood its importance. And he had looked in the mirror since that moment, knowing that the extinction of a species might go against him in the end, and that now the future of that unknown species might rest in a wormhole pod that had sped off into space.

"I am thinking," Romanov said, "that the report I give to Security Officer Casey should describe a technical problem with the guidance software of the twelfth pod. Given his reputation I expect the security officer will not like that answer, but I can ensure you he will accept it—assuming, that is, that he never hears other ideas that might set him to questioning things more deeply."

Torrance's stomach turned. "I understand, sir."

"Do you?" Romanov said, waiting. His eyebrows rose with the question.

Yes, Torrance thought. He understood with total clarity. His career wasn't over, but it was being held hostage. Play the game my way, Romanov was saying, and we both come out ahead. Play it yours and your ass will be drop-kicked into an open air lock as quickly as Security Officer Casey can whisper court-martial into his UG comm phone.

It was okay, he thought.

Romanov was right.

Torrance had done everything he could, more than most would have. The tailfin of that twelfth wormhole pod had enough room for them both to hang their consciences on, and it was time for both of them to wade onward. All he had to do was to formalize the report.

"That could be done, sir," he finally said.

"Then I suggest you make it happen."

"Thank you, sir."

Torrance left the captain's office and walked briskly to the lift tubes.

He had a lot to think about. He had a report to prepare, and he needed to consider what to do with the data files he had filled with signals from the planet. He should also probably consider what to tell Security Officer Casey when he eventually came calling. Romanov may say that he could protect Torrance, but he knew the game better than to think a government security officer would settle for a captain's word when there was more muck to stir.

But mostly, he needed to think about his life. He needed to plan.

He had seven and a half years left aboard *Everguard*. If any man could get back on the promotion path, it was going to be him.

CHAPTER 8

UGIS *Everguard*
Ship Local Date: May 16, 2204
Ship Local Time: 0955

The report took Torrance nearly two hours to create. No, he thought as he submitted it into Romanov's queue, it took nearly two hours to *fabricate*.

He couldn't help but think about the wormhole pod.

What had happened to it? Where was it?

He imagined the twelfth pod, crumpled and derelict on a desolate red planet. He hoped it survived entry, but wasn't sure whether he actually hoped there was anything down there to retrieve it or not. Giving an alien species such a gift was oddly exciting, but doing it under the umbrella of genocide slammed a gigantic door on his enthusiasm.

If it were true, though, if an alien species did live on Eden, and if they found the pod, what then? Would they understand it? Could they work with it? How long would it take them to re-engineer the technology? And, if they did, how long before they did anything about it?

The universe is big, and time is long.

Would he ever learn the truth?

He sat back and rubbed his eyes, knowing Malloy was due any minute. The idea of another meeting right now was about as appealing as an extra round of leadership training.

He glanced again at the screen to his right to see the image of *Sunchaser* there, and couldn't help but choke up a little.

He was tired, and his brain was mush from days of stress, but he would have to be dead to keep his heart from racing at the thought that a mere six hours ago, *Sunchaser*, an Excelsior class cruiser, had been stationed outside the Solar System's asteroid belt, and that now it was in the Alpha Centauri system and running on trim boosters as it edged closer to *Everguard*.

They were far enough from Alpha Centauri A that the admiral had opened the observation hall's shades. A view of *Sunchaser* was high on everyone's list, and in this case "everyone" most certainly included one Lieutenant Commander Torrance Black.

Malloy stepped into his office and gave an appreciative whistle.

"Can you believe it, LC?" Malloy said as he took a seat.

"Incredible, eh?" Torrance replied.

Torrance sat back and thought about what he was going to say.

This was supposed to be a goal-setting session where the two of them focused on preparing for the return flight, but the image of *Sunchaser* made it impossible to concentrate. The air in his office was so stale he struggled to breathe. The idea of digging into electronic system reports, or discussing automatic backups, or doing anything else it took to run the everyday crap that made the ship operational gave him a case of the screaming willies. The thought of discussing routine assignments with Lieutenant Malloy made his brain go floppy.

Duty or not, he was physically incapable of having this conversation.

"What do you say we take twenty and hit the observation deck?" Torrance said.

"I don't suppose I can be court-martialed for following a direct order, can I?"

"Never put anything past Interstellar Command."

Malloy snuffed. "Interstellar Command."

Torrance shrugged. "It's no worse than Solar Command, right?"

"If you say so."

"Let's go." Torrance stood.

The two walked down the corridor.

"Are we really going to get a walk-through?" Malloy asked as they waited for a lift tube.

"That's what I understand. The admiral wants the entire crew to see what next-generation spacecraft look like, so I think it will happen."

Malloy nodded. "Must be nice."

"What's that?"

"To be on a ship so fast you don't have to carry your family along with you just to see them grow up."

Torrance glanced at the lieutenant. Like many of the crew, Malloy didn't have much family left, and none of that aboard the ship.

"Thinking about someone in particular?"

"No," Malloy said. "Not really. But I can't help wondering what it's like back home."

The comment struck Torrance.

Ever since the launch, he hadn't actually been thinking of home at all. He hadn't thought about his parents or Adrienne or anyone else in the Solar System. His entire existence had been absorbed by the signals from Eden. Who made them? What would those creatures be like?

He glanced at the lift tube indicator and realized then exactly what his conversation with Romanov had actually meant.

He wasn't to explore the issue.

He wasn't to look at the data. That data, in fact, wouldn't exist.

Those questions he had been pondering would have no answers. Pondering?

No. He had not been *pondering* these questions. He had been poring over them, obsessing, focusing on them to the exclusion of everything else. This was how he was. Torrance Black did not like story lines with cliff-hangers. He found answers to things. It was why he was good at what he did. He enjoyed the game of bait and chase. The tough work of drilling into details that caused others to lose interest just pushed him harder. Torrance had been so focused on these questions that he hadn't fully considered the ramifications of Captain Romanov's orders.

But now he realized that *Sunchaser*'s arrival was both the fulfillment of a dream and a harbinger of loss. The conflicting ideas left him numb.

He wasn't looking forward to leaving the Centauri system.

For a moment, Torrance was nearly overcome with the need to tell Malloy about his theory of life on Eden, but he snapped out of that quickly. Malloy was connected to the rest of the crew, and he was a talker. Torrance couldn't risk what could happen if Malloy spread it.

At best, Romanov would crap all over his rank, and at worst…well, Torrance didn't want to think about Security Officer Casey. Government officers made him break out. Just the idea of what Casey might do if he found out about the Eden files sent waves of paranoia crawling over his back.

The tube arrived. The door slid open, and they stepped into a compartment with four other people.

"Observation bridge," they all said as the door slid shut.

They shared sheepish glances. The observation bridge was twenty layers up. The sense of added gravity came as the lift rose with a frictionless grace that made Torrance smile.

Every system on this ship was his.

He liked things to run smoothly.

A woman behind them continued a conversation she had clearly been having before the lift picked up Torrance and Malloy. "Executive President Mubadid can't keep the combined congresses in line on this asteroid thing," she said.

"I think she's on her way out," the man beside her replied.

"Good riddance."

"How can *you* say that? She's the one who pushed this mission."

"She's also the one who gave half the asteroid belt to miners."

"It's just a bunch of rocks."

"The asteroid fields are a natural treasure."

Torrance cleared his throat to interrupt.

It wasn't his way to press himself on people outside his command, but he was feeling a different sense of lightness this morning, and the words slipped out almost before he thought them.

"We've got a Star Drive spacecraft off our bow, folks," he said. "What do you say that we not trash the moment, eh?"

The two grew quiet.

Malloy's lips gave a playful uptick.

This one, Torrance knew, would circulate through the crew before third shift. He felt good about that. Despite the enclosed feel of the liftpod, the muscles along his neck relaxed.

He wasn't surprised that the two were arguing, though.

Sunchaser brought the crew everything from fresh fruit to new technology—but mostly it brought news from home that wasn't two and a half years old. So most of the crew was now drunk on information, and—unlike Torrance, who preferred to take time to absorb any situation—they wanted to talk about it.

The most popular bits of news were holo-vids of *Sunchaser* departing on the first Star Drive flight ever. The clips showed the craft lighting its engines, then streaking out of sight leaving an image behind that was half ghost, half firework rocket. They showed its scientists collecting data from Barnard's Star on that maiden voyage, then returning to base.

But the news also included stories about everything from a three-year drought that had struck Asian rice fields, to political issues like the use of the asteroid belt and the clamor over the United Government leasing Europa's mineral rights to DelpCo Energy, which planned to turn Jupiter's most famous moon's icy landscape into a transport refueling station.

Torrance was amused to hear the Chicago Cubs had lost the Solar Series after New Zealand's Karen Lashley hit a grand slam in the top of the eighth to take the seventh game 12-10.

The lift came to a stop, and the door slid open.

Torrance had read Excelsior's spec sheets. He had seen news clips and video segments, and pored through the program's technical directives. He had devoured every white paper on multidimensional matter transfer he could find.

But nothing could have prepared him for this.

Sunchaser filled the entire observation panel.

Goosebumps spread over Torrance's arms, and a shit-eating grin smeared itself all over his face.

She was built in three portions: a sleek central fore-cabin that housed the inner workings of the Star Drive itself, and two smaller pods behind and below it—one housing the crew, the other holding the bridge and operational offices. The entire package looked like a bi-leveled delta wing, and seemed to split vacuum even as it was sitting still.

"It's the most beautiful thing I've ever seen," Torrance said as he came to the window.

Everguard's crew filled the observation deck. They stared and pointed, speaking as if they were in a museum.

"We did it, eh, LC?" Malloy elbowed him.

Torrance put his hand on the lieutenant's shoulder.

"Yeah, Karl. We did it. We really did it."

A bay door slid back from the middle of *Sunchaser*'s central cabin, and a voice piped over *Everguard*'s shipwide intercom.

"Shuttles Azure and Black preparing for rendezvous, *Everguard*."

A shuttle nosed from *Sunchaser*'s bay.

"Roger, *Sunchaser*. We are prepared to receive visitors."

A cheer rose.

Chapter 9

UGIS *Everguard*
Ship Local Date: May 16, 2204
Ship Local Time: 2255

In order to be sure Silvio was there, Torrance checked the duty roster before returning to the Signal Processing Lab.

Torrance could have done the file manipulation at any time, but he had something else on his mind now. With the exception of Captain Romanov, Silvio Nivead was the only person on the ship who could suggest Torrance had an interest in life on the second planet. He wanted to find out if maybe Silvio could be made to see the value of keeping that bit of information to himself.

So he arrived at the lab late in the shift.

Silvio was standing at a multidimensional holographic display, studying what appeared to be an interleaved pairing of emissions from the three stars in the system.

"LC, long time no sees." His grin was big and gap-toothed.

"I couldn't stay away," Torrance replied as he took a workstation.

"We have to stop meeting this way, my friend."

"But then what would I have to look forward to all day?"

Silvio's laugh was more of a bray.

"What brings you down?" he said. "Taking more orders?"

"Orders?"

"You're the pizza guy, right?" the cheeky bastard said.

Torrance laughed despite himself.

"Maybe we should call you LC Supreme, eh? Or do you prefer LC Pepperoni?"

"I'm more a sausage and onions guy myself."

"Lieutenant Commander Sausage and Onions." Nivead shrugged. "Doesn't have the same ring."

"Story of my life."

Torrance got to work typing commands.

"Abke," he said to the shipboard computer at the same time. "I need you to retrieve emissions files A-Planet-1 and A-Planet-2 I was previously studying. Also grab all the residual elements and reports I pulled in the early morning of local date May 6 of this year."

"Time period?"

"Let's say 0230 to 0530," he replied.

"Files retrieved."

He finished keying in commands that would package those files into a sub-block. Then he renamed that sub-block and stashed it in the trash system where he could find it later.

"Please delete all analytics and roll back all source files to previous state."

"Analytics deleted."

"Thank you."

"Which discard protocol would you like, sir?"

"Standard," Torrance said.

Standard protocol would mean the files would be held in process and shredded with all others at the end of the day as the scheduled maintenance bots fired. It gave him an hour to pull the sub-block, which should be enough time.

"No more pizza?" Silvio said.

"Turns out there's no delivery in this area code," he quipped back.

"Sons of a bitches," Nivead replied. "Isn't that always the way?"

Torrance got up and went to Silvio's station, examining the multicolor display. "What are you working on?"

Silvio stared at Torrance, clearly trying to see what the LC had up his sleeve.

"I'm just interested," Torrance said, hoping he didn't sound too defensive.

"Not many folks who say that actually mean it, Squanto."

Torrance peered into the mix that the projector had created as a column of multihued lights.

"Looks like frequency patterns."

"Good eye, LC."

He checked the system settings. They were arranged to show Silvio the interplay between the spectral densities of each star's metallic elements as their orbits progressed. Despite being the largest of the three, Alpha Centauri A was the least metallic at only two times the the mass of Sol in non-hydrogem or helium compounds. Alpha Centauri B carried nearly two and a half times Sol's mass, and tiny Proxima was somewhere in the middle.

"Metallicity games?" Torrance said.

"Playing with a theory," Silvio replied. "We got lots of time for that down here, you know?"

The time scale of the model moved forward, and the patterns shifted.

Torrance wasn't sure how to take Silvio's comment.

"What's the theory?"

Silvio laughed. "A wild-haired idea about where the three came from. Nothing to be too excited about. You know how wild-haired ideas are, right, LC?"

Torrance gave him an inquisitive glance.

"Yes, Silvio," he said. "I think we both know how wild-haired ideas are."

"Like pizza delivery in space, right?"

Torrance nodded then, understanding that Silvio Nivead was telling him that his secret was safe as long as Torrance played straight with him, that guys like Nivead had less use for government security officers poking around their stuff than Torrance did himself.

Perhaps he shouldn't have worried, but Torrance got the idea that under Nivead's rugged shell there was another factor playing. Silvio was a sharp guy, a guy who knew how things worked but whose career had been stalled from the very beginning by a combination of things outside of his control. By now his reputation was built thick with sarcasm, but Torrance wondered if, at one time, the engineer had greater ideas about how his life would end up—if perhaps he had wild-haired visions of himself doing something bigger than sitting late-shift on *Everguard*.

He spent another five minutes actually enjoying the process of letting Silvio explain his idea. Then Torrance left the processing lab and returned to his quarters where he most definitely did not use his private access or his systems security privileges to access *Everguard*'s digital trash system. Nor did he extricate the sub-block that he had earlier renamed, or scrub certain registries to remove record of his actions. And when he wasn't complete with those tasks, he most certainly did not ever place that sub-block into a set of newly renamed files in his own personal and secure memory space.

When the sub-block was not extracted, and the files were not open, Torrance didn't then spend the next three hours playing with their contents. And when he was finished with that, he almost certainly did not create a white-noise file from the emissions stream from Eden that he then looped endlessly as he fell asleep.

Anyone who said such a thing had happened was merely partaking in a wild-haired game.

At least, that's what he would say.

If anyone ever asked.

What is beyond doubt, however, is that Torrance *did* wake up early the next morning, bleary-eyed but oddly invigorated. And after he showered he cleaned up the data path he might have left, storing away files, running an atomic-level cleanse routine, and closing his private system—locking it under both his personal and his systems keys.

Just to be safe.

CHAPTER 10

UGIS *Everguard*
Ship Local Date: May 17, 2204
Ship Local Time: 1800

Torrance had never liked parties.

He could handle them well enough, he supposed. He could talk with anyone, and people seemed to laugh at his jokes. But he never really saw the point. Parties were superficial. They took him away from things he would rather be doing—which right now meant figuring out how to dig through the Eden files he had placed into his private memory space. Beyond that, parties left him feeling uncomfortable, like he was lacking in some way.

So, as usual, the celebration was in full swing as he entered the observation deck, a shade later than the norm.

The place looked like a gaudy combination of a high school mixer and a political convention.

Music from a real quartet played in the background.

An upside-down sea of silvered ribbons hung from the ceiling, glimmering blue and purple with lights that were attached to the wall by jaunty arms that made them look like they were robotic eyeballs of some kind of mechanical spider. The ribbons moved with the room's ventilation, and made the place feel like a postmodern star factory created by a computer that had been programmed to merge the dreams of Pollock and van Gogh.

The crew milled about beneath the field of light, talking and drinking, huddling in cliques that pretended they were not cliques. The jumbled drone of their stories formed a wall of white noise that vibrated in the pit of his stomach. The enclosure was thick with the aroma of steamed vegetables and stewing meats, and warm with the heat of bodies. The admiral's table sat at the head of the room, raised on a platform and draped in white cloth.

Open bars lined the back of the hall.

The observation deck's screen remained open, so the thrill-inducing presence of *Sunchaser* alongside the now-archaic *Everguard* stood in silent testimony that the galaxy, and maybe the universe, was now theirs.

The wormholes were set.

The last seven and a half years of their lives had been a success, and now the crew was celebrating.

Yes, Torrance thought, the party was in full swing.

"Hey! Here he is!" Malloy called.

Torrance felt a slap on his back.

Like Torrance, Malloy wore his dress whites with silver piping. Unlike Torrance, however, his collar was open, the tips turned out and downward. His gloved hands held a box wrapped in white paper with silver ribbon. He turned and motioned to people at a table across the room. Torrance recognized his team.

"Come on!" Mallory's voice boomed. "I found him."

His crew gathered around.

"What's all this about?" Torrance said.

"We've got a little something for you, LC."

"You didn't have to do that."

"You're not getting off that easy," Malloy replied. He waited until the gang had settled.

"My friends," he called, "we have come to bury Torrance Black, not to praise him…er…praise him, not to…ah, whatever."

The gathering laughed, their cheeks flush with champagne.

Malloy spoke again. "In all sincerity, I want to take this time to say that Lieutenant Commander Black has been a fine man to work for during this launch. He kept his head, and he kept us focused. And unlike most the folks who give the orders around here, we all know he can do real work."

The team cheered at this, and Torrance actually smiled.

"It was his idea to look for outside influences a second time—without which, I should remind everyone, we would probably still be in the command center looking at schematics."

Another round of laughter and a few raised glasses came.

Malloy turned to Torrance.

"Given all that, sir, we thought you might appreciate a little something to remember the event by." He proffered the package.

Torrance took it amid a smattering of applause.

"I don't know what to say," he mumbled.

Heat rose to his cheeks. He had gotten used to people congratulating him in the hallways and commenting to him in the mess. But those were simple things. Having the crew he worked so closely with do something like this made the world seem claustrophobically small, but also made him remarkably lighthearted.

"Open it up, LC," Ensign Whalen said.

Torrance tore the paper, found a box inside, and lifted the lid.

It was a square slab of the composite EMI shielding they had used to wrap the launch chambers—engraved with the image of a wormhole pod in flight. In the distance was a blazing sun, Alpha Centauri A. The words *UGIS Everguard, Changing the Universe* were engraved along the top of the slab. The ship's date and time of the launch were on the bottom.

He looked up to see the smiling faces of the entire team staring at him with anticipation.

"This is the coolest damned thing I've ever seen," he said.

"We've got all our names on the back, sir."

He turned it over.

"Then I'll have to display it on this side," he quipped, holding it up so everyone could view their names.

The crew laughed, and everything felt right.

This presentation meant as much to them as it did to him. The idea took him by surprise. This was a night for laughter, he thought. As much as he hated parties, it was a night to breathe.

"Thank you all very much," he said. "Seriously. I don't want to get all mushy because we still have, uh, a few years of time left together. But you guys were a great team. Are a great team. I think we should give ourselves a cheer."

"LC's right," Malloy said, raising his glass. "On three. One, two, three.”

They all cheered. Then again, and again.

Finally they each shook Torrance’s hand and drifted back to their own tables.

“Hey, LC?” Malloy said. “Do you know Lieutenant Harthing?”

Malloy moved his hands in such a way as to present a woman who had come to stand beside him. Torrance recognized her.

The lieutenant was radiant in her formal blues with a silver sash cinched at the waist. She was thin, maybe to the point of awkwardness. His age, he thought. From her bearing, he suspected she spent a good deal of time in the ship’s gymnasium. A pair of blue barrettes pulled her hair back in a graceful sweep around the back of her head. Silvered earrings glittered from her lobes. Her makeup was a spare application of coloring to her lips and something to augment her eyes. The effect was dazzling, though.

He recalled her name on the roster of officers in the Forward Nav office, but that was as far as it went.

Torrance blushed. Harthing seemed equally stymied.

“Only by reputation,” Torrance finally said, taking her gloved hand. “Which is, of course, quite good.”

“This is Lieutenant Commander Black,” Malloy said to her. “He’s a real steady guy. I thought the two of you might hit it off.”

The three stood there for an awkward moment.

“Hello,” Torrance said, suddenly finding himself annoyed at Malloy, both for putting him in a situation he wasn’t prepared for and for the tone in his voice when he called Torrance a “steady guy.”

“You can just call me Torrance,” he said.

“Marisa,” Harthing said. “Nice to meet you. Congratulations on your launch.”

“Thank you. You’re navigation, right?”

“Yes, I’m surprised you knew.”

Malloy chimed in. “When he’s not writing wormhole code, LC is the service engineer. He knows everything about everyone.”

They laughed, but Torrance grimaced.

“Not everything,” he said.

He couldn’t help a glance across the room where Security Officer Casey was speaking with Sunchaser’s First Officer. The idea of an overseer made him nervous enough as it was, and it didn't help matters that Casey caught his eye, smiled, and raised his wineglass in an "I've got plans for you" kind of way that Torrance found himself imagining as a threat.

"I see another glass of champagne with my name on it," Malloy said. "I'll leave you two kids to chat."

So they chatted.

"Karl said you've been in the service for a long time."

Torrance nodded. "It's how I went to school, actually."

"I guess you could say the same for me, too. But I've always dreamed of being in space, too. This was the safest way to do that."

A server bot streamed past with a tray of champagne.

"Drink?" Torrance asked.

She smiled, and he grabbed two from the tray. The wine was sweet.

"Tell me about the launch," she said. "I bet it was the coolest thing ever."

"To be honest, I'm just happy it's over."

She gave half a laugh. "I bet."

She had a catch in her voice that he liked, and grace to her movements that he found mesmerizing. She used her hands when she talked, which made a conversation with her like watching a ballet. She was military through and through. Her father and mother were stationed on Venus Command, working security detail for the science station there. They had traveled all her life, so this stint on *Everguard* was the longest she had ever been in one environment. She valued structure, maybe even more than he did. She understood the discipline of a system that worked on checks and guards.

Torrance liked her eyes and the way she asked questions that led to interesting ideas.

She asked Torrance if he danced, and though he didn't really, he also didn't want to disappoint her. Somehow he managed to not break her toes.

Remarkably, the party was over before he knew it, and he was both shocked and a little dismayed when the lights to the assembly hall went up.

"Can I walk you home?" he asked.

She smiled and they left the deck together.

* * *

Torrance and Marisa strode along the hallway, her hand resting lightly inside the crook of his elbow. It was three in the morning. The deck was quiet.

"This is my stop," she said, pointing toward the door. It was a standard-issue four-bay quarters. She hesitated, then slipped her hand from his elbow. "I would invite you in, but I don't want to wake anyone up."

"That's all right."

A few strands of her hair had slipped from the barrettes, and her sash was rumpled from the dance. He could see she was as tired as he was. But otherwise Marisa was still as stunning as she had been earlier.

"Yes?" she said, obviously sensing he wanted to say something.

"I was just thinking that maybe you would like to do something else together sometime." The words came out before he could stop them, which is probably why they worked well enough.

Her smile brightened. "That would be great."

Torrance smiled, too.

He bent and kissed her. Marisa kissed him back.

Then she smiled and pressed her palm to the door's scanner. It slid open and she stepped into her room.

"Call me," she said over her shoulder.

The door shut behind her, and Torrance leaned against the corridor bulkhead.

It had been a very long time since he had felt so good.

Chapter 11

UGIS *Everguard*
Ship Local Date: May 19, 2204
Ship Local Time: 1200

A blast from the snare drum echoed through the loading bay.

Torrance stood at the end of a long line of officers, his back straight and his arms loosely at his sides. The chamber was cavernous relative to most of the ship, big enough that the drumming reverberated against the stark metal walls, large enough that it was cold despite the gathering of warm bodies all together. It smelled lightly of metal and dust despite the cleaning bots that ran through the place earlier. He logged an entry to his register of things to do: *check janitorial for maintenance status*. The ventilation system was running hard enough that Torrance also noted to accelerate its next maintenance cycle.

Admiral Hatch entered the hallway with his full entourage.

His uniform was pristine and sharply creased, his shoulders square, his jodhpurs flared, and the corners of his collar achingly stiff. He carried a staff under one arm—a meter-long shaft of dark mahogany polished in warm brown tones with bronze casings capping both ends.

The band brought the music up as he made his way into the main bay and began to parade down the line of *Everguard*'s officers.

Romanov stood at attention near the shuttle.

The admiral made his way slowly down the line, shaking hands with his staff and leaning in to speak directly into their ears.

Torrance couldn't help but feel the moment.

He swallowed hard, and was surprised when his mind flashed on a memory of his dad standing in front of his bathroom mirror one day when Torrance was just a kid.

Torrance clutched a datapad with his model of the Delta rocket. He had pulled plans from archive data and painstakingly put them into the computer. It had taken days to figure out what parts were missing, and another three weeks of late nights to find models that would recreate the full system. When he was done, he had put it all into a virtual engine and launched it. The thing blew up, of course. Fifteen times. But the sixteenth shot was the one.

He made it into orbit—at least that's what the math said.

"That's mighty fine," his dad said, rubbing his day-old stubble and pushing his white work shirt into his trousers. He looked into the mirror and adjusted his tie. He hadn't even looked at the display. "I'm glad it worked."

"I'm going to make spaceships someday," Torrance said.

His dad got a loopy grin on his face.

"I think your mom would rather you stay home."

"I'm serious, Dad. I'm going to make something big."

His dad turned from the mirror and drank down the last of his morning coffee.

"I'm late for work," he said.

Then he looked at Torrance and saw what was almost certainly a frown of disappointment on his face.

"Sure, Torrance. It's great that you want to make something like that. But don't be too worried if that doesn't happen, all right. The world is tough, you know? Sometimes it's best not to dream too big."

Torrance snapped out of the memory, tasting bitterness against the back of his throat.

Kip Levitt was in the audience, too.

Levitt's dark skin was smooth and made the crisp white formals seem even whiter.

His dad had been right in some ways.

Sometimes life was just one sucker punch after another.

But the people in this room had been part of something that might someday be argued was the single most important event in human history. Right this minute, Admiral Hatch was going home to make the purpose of the *Everguard* mission a reality. And Torrance had been part of it.

A bit part, maybe, but a part.

He had done something important.

Hadn't he?

And yet …

He glanced again at Kip Levitt.

Then at Captain Romanov.

Then at Government Security Officer Casey.

The juxtaposition of his emotions was a strange mix as the admiral drew forward to salute Casey, then made his way down the row of his staff officers.

The music drew to its close as Hatch finished his last handshake and came to stand before Captain Romanov.

A whirlwind of conflict crashed inside Torrance's brain, and for an instant, he thought he was actually going to cry. Damned silly of him, he supposed.

"Are you prepared to receive command, sir?" the admiral barked.

"Aye, sir."

Hatch proffered the staff, and Romanov took it.

"Sir," the admiral said boldly. "I give *Everguard* to your safekeeping. Sail well, Captain Romanov, she is a fine ship."

"I accept your command, Admiral. I hope only to serve as competently as you have."

Applause filled the bay, and the band played again.

Romanov gave a formal salute, which the admiral returned.

Hatch leaned in to whisper something private to the captain, and Romanov grinned with teeth as white as his uniform. He nodded and patted the admiral on the forearm. A moment later the admiral strode into his waiting shuttle. Then the door closed, and the order to evacuate the vacuum chamber was given.

With that, *Everguard* closed its doors to visitors for the final time.

Starsling

CHAPTER 12

UGIS *Everguard*
Ship Local Date: May 21, 2204
Ship Local Time: 1255

Romanov's voice was firm over the communications system.

"We are go for star sling. Roll ninety dark-side."

This is it, Torrance thought.

They were going to drive the collider system as hard as she could go and dive toward Alpha Centauri A. This would catch the star's gravitational well and, with the right application of power, would slingshot *Everguard* away as if the ship was a comet from Centauri's own version of the Oort cloud. The maneuver would bring them much closer to the star than before and expose the shielded bottom of the craft to its severe energies.

They had made the same maneuver on their way here—a slingshot around Sol that increased their velocity and sped them along a proper course, but that first loop had been made around a star that was slightly smaller than Alpha Centauri A. The same maneuver here meant a steeper rise in temperature and higher stresses on an older ship.

It also meant this was the most dangerous moment of the entire mission.

Everguard's underside was shaped to shed heat, and its cooling system was a simple steady-state device reliable enough that

Torrance wasn't concerned about its survival, but the collider struts and the ring were another story.

The standard EVA visual inspections had been completed and passed prior to the wormhole pod launch, as had all the proper routine maintenance activities. But the struts were older now. They would be under heavy load, and since shielding for these areas could not be efficiently formed, the situation called for an active monitoring system capable of sensing minute thermal changes and providing immediate streams of supercoolant. One blooming hot spot and *Everguard* would disintegrate.

It was his team's job to monitor and report, and if anything went wrong it would be his team's job to fix it before the worst hit.

Numbers flashed on the monitors in his office.

The time was spot-on: 1300 hours.

They had been accelerating toward the star since morning. Assuming everything held together, they would be heading for home in just over three hours.

Torrance strolled around the engineering pit outside his office, trying to remain casual as *Everguard* rolled to expose its heat shields to the star.

There wasn't much he could do at this point beyond be there with his crew as they worked, which they did with professional calm that said they knew how much could go wrong.

The ship's artificial gravity system made adjustments so *Everguard*'s maneuver felt somewhat motionless, but Ensign Hallie Whalen had built a simple monitor of the process on the corner of her desktop—placing a steel bearing on a translucent purple air pillow. As the ship neared perigee, *Everguard*'s angular momentum would increase the effective gravity inside the ship. The stronger field would pull the steel ball further into the pillow. A betting pool sprang up wherein each crew member guessed what the max deflection would wind up being.

Torrance decided he liked Whalen early in the trip. She was one of those people who had a silent intelligence about them, someone who could do just about anything she set her mind to but she wasn't obnoxious about it. She was someone who just went about doing her job.

"How's the bearing, Hallie?" Torrance asked.

Whalen glanced at the air pillow. "Down a hundredth, LC."

"Anyone have twenty-two hundredths?"

"No, sir."

Torrance grinned. "Put me down for a ten spot."

"You got it, LC."

Torrance patted her on her shoulder and continued his stroll, trying not to think about the stresses that were building up in the collider struts, trying to ignore the g forces he knew the ship was being exposed to, and the heat that would vaporize them if the heat channels somehow failed.

He thought about Marisa.

Being navigation command, she would be busy right now, but he imagined her fingers running over her station, occasionally brushing hair out of her eyes as she, too, worked with the calm efficiency of someone who knew their job.

What would become of the two of them?

It felt strange to care.

He shook his head and glanced around the room, then to Whalen's purple pillow.

It was down three-hundredths.

Nineteen more and he was a winner.

Four hours later *Everguard* had traversed Alpha Centauri A and was heading home.

"That's it," Torrance said to his team. "Stand down the mission."

There was no big celebration this time. Despite the fact that completion of star sling was easily as noteworthy as launching the pods, the crew had only smug smiles and relieved sighs to pass to each other.

They'd made it.

"It's all vacuum from here," Malloy quipped.

The team laughed.

"Well, Mr. Malloy. Looks like you can afford to be jovial," Whalen said.

Everyone paused.

She brought her gaze up from the bearing and pillow.

"You've got eighteen-hundredths, right?"

Malloy grinned. "I guess the first round is on me," he said.

Finally, the group cheered.

* * *

The invitation was in Torrance's system when he returned to his desk.

66

CHAPTER 13

UGIS *Everguard*
Ship Local Date: May 21, 2204
Ship Local Time: 1715

To: Black, Torrance, LCMD
From: Casey, Malcolm, Government Security Officer, Everguard
SUBJ: Debrief

Content:
I would like to speak with you regarding the launch and subsequent flight path of wormhole pod #12.

An invitation to a meeting the next day was attached.

Torrance touched *"Accept."*

As if there had been any choice.

Chapter 14

UGIS *Everguard*
Ship Local Date: May 22, 2204
Ship Local Time: 1330

The security officer stood as Torrance stepped into Malcolm Casey's office.

Casey was a svelte, well-conditioned man of average height. His hands were long for his size, and his dark hair was thinning as it receded. He wore a tailored beige jump jacket trimmed in navy. A pair of matching navy pants gave a formal edge to his faux casual appearance. The outfit gave Casey the air of a man trying to be younger than he was, but the entire package gave an awkward and dangerous edge to his sense of command.

"Thank you for being prompt," Casey said.

"You're welcome, sir."

Torrance needed to get through this conversation without Casey learning about the Eden files he had stored away—a thing Torrance was fairly sure he could accomplish. All he had to do was stick to the report—which he had read often enough since the summons that he thought he could quote it verbatim. But actually being in Casey's office, which was permeated with the aura of real power, made his brain run in a series of endless loops. It was suddenly harder to breathe. The palms of his hands grew damp while the doorway cycled shut behind him with a finality that multiplied his discomfort.

"Please take a seat." Casey motioned to the padded chair that sat before his desk.

Torrance cleared his throat and sat down.

Casey waited until Torrance got as comfortable as he was going to get.

The office was cold, a fact that was a running joke in the shipboard systems command, but otherwise it seemed no different from any other officer's space. A curved projection screen fit into the corner to Torrance's right, and the security officer's desk was the same clear surface that Romanov's had, a surface complete with an interactive layer that could be used as a display, or to project photons into a form of holographic output—though in Casey's case, the display was shrouded in the pure noise that was indecipherable to anyone without the proper implants.

Torrance's gaze went to the rounded sensor pod in the far corner.

It was one of three e-lint transmitter shields installed in the office. Together they comprised an electronic intelligence system that made it impossible for conversations inside the office to be overheard by most sensors in existence. It wouldn't block devices inside the shell, though. Torrance knew that every element of this conversation was being recorded, including most of Torrance's vital signs and the tonal qualities of his voice as he replied.

"I read your report regarding the stray wormhole pod," Casey finally said.

"Captain Romanov said you would."

"I'm sure he did."

Torrance swallowed, and put his hands into his lap, waiting for Casey to continue. He cleared his throat again, wondering where this was going.

"Could you describe for me what you think happened?"

"It's all in the report, sir," Torrance said.

"I would like to hear it in your own words."

"I'm not trying to hide anything, sir."

"I'm sure that is the case, Lieutenant Commander."

"Thank you," Torrance said. He knew Casey would ask these questions, but it was different dealing with them in person than thinking about how he should answer them when he was by himself. "To be completely honest, no one can say with one hundred percent certainty what the issue was, but it seems obvious that the guidance software had a bug in its calibration."

Casey leaned forward. "Perhaps you could educate me. Why didn't that kind of error affect every pod?"

"That's a good question, sir. In some cases it would do just that. The cals...uh, calibrations...are loaded from the central memory unit, and every pod should get the same one."

"And that didn't happen this time?"

"Yes, that did happen. We checked the loading routine, the wiring paths, and the calibrations themselves. It's clear the system loaded each pod the same."

Torrance's gaze went to the e-lint pod and flickered back. He rubbed his palms against his pant legs. So far he had not had to lie.

"What happened, then?"

Torrance cleared his throat again, and the sound served to make him even more uncomfortable. Casey was going a little off script.

Casey gave a relaxed smile. "It's all right, Lieutenant Commander. I'm sure you haven't done anything wrong, and if you haven't done anything wrong, you won't have anything to hide, right?"

Torrance's throat constricted. He hated that argument.

"Yes, sir."

Casey sat back in his chair, crossed one leg over the other, and gazed at him in contemplation. He motioned the question again with one long-fingered hand. "So?"

"As I said," Torrance replied. "We can't say anything with absolute certainty. Either the cal didn't load properly, or the pod had a hardware failure. I'm calling it a software problem because the system's hardware passed multiple tests prior to both launch attempts."

"What are the chances that someone adjusted the parameters after the calibrations were loaded?"

Torrance paused and cocked his head as if in thought.

It was a gesture he did often, and one he had practiced several times since receiving Casey's summons. He spoke his words now in that same, slow way he had practiced. It felt better, he thought, to be back into a conversational flow he had prepared for.

"It's not completely impossible, sir. But it would be very hard to do. It would have to come from outside the system as a whole, and it would probably leave some fairly obvious tracks that I would have seen—things like access registers in various logs."

"And you do not see these accesses on the logs now?"

"No," Torrance said, trying to remain calm as he spoke his prepared phrase. "There are no accesses on the registries when I look at them."

The room fell to a silent pinpoint.

This was the critical moment. Torrance struggled to keep his heart from racing. He had loaded the final calibration from a remote system, and had gone in and cleaned the registers immediately after launch. It was important that Casey not pick up on the truth here. Get through this step of the conversation, and both Torrance and Romanov should be in clear sailing.

Casey tapped his index and middle finger against one arm of the chair.

"You are probably right," he said. "Though, I admit that I have wondered if it was possible that you, yourself, could have sabotaged the system. However, I keep hitting two points that make me doubt you would do something as egregious as sabotage a mission-critical pod."

Torrance waited.

"First, I can't see a motive. I can't figure out why you would do it. I mean, you're an engineer. What benefit would you have for taking that kind of risk? None, right? I mean, beyond the pure fancy of seeing that it could be done, I suppose."

Casey's gaze fell on him.

"I'm not really that kind of geek, sir."

"Yes," Casey said. "That is reason number two. Your career has been a fairly simple one. Stable, right? Or maybe *unremarkable* is a better descriptor. You've never been one to step too far out of line, and never one to take on half-baked ideas. So the second barrier I have to thinking you would actually do this kind of thing is that you have never been bold enough to perpetuate such an act before."

Torrance felt the insult in Casey's voice.

"I'm not sure what to say, sir."

"On the other hand—" Casey's eyes drew tighter and his gaze

became laserlike. A chill came to the back of Torrance's neck. "—there is the fact that you recently learned you did not make the promotion list."

Torrance swallowed, and gripped the arms of his chair. He didn't expect this turn. Heat rose to his cheeks and forehead.

"That is true, sir. I did learn that."

"And you're not upset."

"I'm disappointed. Of course I am. But what does that have to do with the wormhole pod?"

Casey hesitated then broke into an overly large smile that was animated enough to say the point of this conversation was at its end.

"You're right, Lieutenant Commander. It is probably unrelated."

Torrance caught the *probably* exactly as he was sure Casey meant him to.

"But it is important to remember that there are those who would exult to see us fail, Torrance. Never discount that fact."

"I won't, sir."

"And you can rest assured that I will not allow that to happen on my watch."

Casey waited, assessing Torrance.

In that moment Torrance understood exactly the game that was being played. Casey was telling Torrance that the security officer had too much at stake to accept returning to the Solar System with a black mark on his record. He was still a young enough man that *Everguard* wouldn't be his last assignment. He expected a bigger play next time around. And Casey was telling Torrance that he didn't believe his story, but couldn't find anything to take him down with. Not yet, anyway. But the government security officer wasn't happy, and he wasn't finished. Torrance could almost hear the message on Casey's gaze. Be careful, Casey was telling him. Be very careful.

He swallowed.

"I understand," Torrance replied.

Casey smiled and sat up slightly.

"I thank you for your time today, Lieutenant Commander. I think you can return to your post."

Casey stood to dismiss him.

"You're welcome, sir," Torrance replied, also standing. "Thank you for your time, too. I understand how important your time is."

"Have a very good shift."

Later that night, Torrance stood in his office scanning the system controls.

He was alone now.

The command was second-shift quiet, just the occasional low voice from the hallways or the nearly silent creaking *Everguard* made when she thought no one was listening.

Torrance listened, though.

He knew this ship inside and out. He understood it.

The low buzz of a power system hummed in the background as he ran his fingers along the bottom of his data screen.

Marisa had asked if he wanted to see a vid, but he begged off, telling her he was tired. "You have a good time, though," he said to make sure she left him alone. They had seen each other three times since the party, and he most certainly wanted to see her again. But, while he *was* tired, that wasn't why he begged off now.

This thing with Casey had him unsettled.

All day long, the government security officer's warnings kept worming their way through his thoughts, making his mind spin loops upon loops, and do flip-flops on top of flip-flops. The line that kept boiling up surprised him, though.

"*... you have never been bold enough to perpetuate such an act.*"

He replayed that line over and over, and every time he did his stomach clenched at the way Casey had taken extra time to draw out the word *bold*.

It was an ugly word.

But it was, he realized, a true word.

The phrase *never been bold enough* was the story of his life.

Lieutenant Commander Torrance Black was intelligent, dependable, and diligent, but he had never been bold like Kip Levitt was bold. He had never stood up for things in the way Kip Levitt had stood up for them.

He had never taken a direct action to make a difference.

Until now.

He paused to sigh, thinking about the Eden files, then created a tri-key secure channel to his private space and called up a data segment that was resident there, thinking of the wormhole pod and thinking about the planet.

Who was there? What were they like?

He scanned the registers where he had stashed the EMI scans.

These data files were important to him.

He wanted to see them again: he wanted to play with them, to spend time understanding them. To really see something in piles of data, he needed to swim in it for a while. The files were the reason he had begged off Marisa's invitation. He was idiot enough to have not really realized it until right now. But he thought about Romanov's warning, and he recalled the edge on Casey's voice. If either of them found out about him cracking open this data, things could get bad in ways he didn't want to imagine. Yet, the data did sing to him, and the words *never been bold enough* prodded at his gut.

This was how it was going to be, he thought. From now on the only way he could work with the files would be to find quiet time when he was by himself. He took a deep sigh, and set himself.

"Abke," he said, "get me the A-2 file, spun to a point two hours prior to the first attempt to launch the wormhole pod. Split the data into one-minute segments."

Bold, he thought as he waited for Abke to finish.

I'll show you bold.

A list of new segments appeared on the display.

"Files prepared," Abke said.

He touched the first. Information flashed in the space above his desk.

It was beautiful in a very real way—sensual, as essential as oxygen, or food, or merely that infinite thing that happened inside him when he looked into deep space.

Torrance needed this.

He needed to understand.

He reached out to touch a column of the feedback spectrum …

"Hey?"

Torrance nearly jumped out of his skin.

Marisa stood in the doorway, one hand on the door, the other propped against her waist.

"I'm sorry!" she said.

Torrance killed his file and turned to face her.

"What'cha doing?" she asked.

"I thought you were going to a vid?"

She crossed her arms at her waist and leaned a shoulder against the bulkhead. Her feet crossed at the ankle.

"Decided there might be better options."

She hadn't seen what he was looking at, which was good. Once that idea settled, he smiled.

He noticed the slant of her smile then, and her white dress with its orange and yellow pattern that fell from her shoulders to wrap around her thin waist.

He couldn't help but be interested.

Something was different for him now.

The decision to look at the files wasn't just a spur-of-the-moment thing, not just a knee-jerk reaction to Casey's threat. The decision to dig into the Eden files was, instead, something that his mind had been struggling with for days. Now that he had made up his mind, though, things clicked. He felt good about it. Studying them would take time, but that was all right. Time—as both Romanov and Casey had so directly insinuated—was the one thing he had a lot of. Now, rather than stressing out over whether to work with the files or not, he realized the right question was how he could do it without being caught.

The change made him feel…well…

"Have I ever told you that you look good in your casuals?" he said.

"This old thing?" she said, gesturing to her dress.

"Yes," he said as he stepped around the desk to stand before her, "that old thing."

He kissed her then.

He put an arm around her, and brought her close and kissed her.

She melted into him, giving as good as she got, and wrapped her arm around his waist. Her touch on the small of his back was light, but noticeable.

"What did you have in mind?" he said.

"What's that?"

"You said there might be better options."

"Well," she sighed. "I was going to invite you to my quarters, but the roommates decided to have a little pinochle party."

"I take it you don't play pinochle?"

"Not when I can avoid it."

He made an expression that confirmed her position.

"Well," he said. "We could go to my quarters."

She smiled. "I suppose we could."

"I have to warn you that I don't play pinochle, either."

"Oh, no," she said as she rose up to kiss him again. "Whatever shall we do, then?"

As they left his office, Torrance smirked to himself.

How's that for bold, he thought.

The Long Leg Home

Chapter 15

UGIS *Everguard*
Ship Local Date: June 12, 2204
Ship Local Time: 0755

As was his norm, Torrance entered Systems Command five minutes before he was due.

"Morning, LC," Ensign Yarrow said.

He raised his coffee to her. "Morning."

Everguard had been accelerating for nearly a month, and the crew was settled back into its routine. The shipboard systems all flashed their status on the displays built into the wall outside his office.

As he did every morning, Torrance started the day by checking his workstation. His desk was raised to the standing position, which in the early stages of his shift was his preference—he sat only when he had visitors or sometimes later in the day, but standing worked better for him much of the time. He put his coffee container on the panel and scanned the reports.

Fifteen work orders had come in during third shift.

"Hot time in Alpha Centauri city," he muttered.

Fifteen. Were these people whaling on equipment for the pure fun of it?

He reordered the list by type.

"Abke, please assign items one through seven to janitorial.

Number eight goes to power systems, ten through fifteen to Petty Officer Olissy in electrical. I'll take nine, myself."

"Assignments made," Abke replied.

He took a deep swallow of his coffee. The caffeine had a hell of a job to do this morning—he was fried from three straight late evenings with Marisa.

Not that he was complaining.

Not a damned bit.

It had been a long time since he had actually wanted to spend time with someone else, and Marisa was fantastic. Thinking about her got him…uh…interested. The light aroma of her hair, the way her eyes grew wide when she was talking about something she was absorbed in, the quirk that came to the corner of her mouth when she was tired of talking. The memory of the touch of her skin against his made him grin.

No, he was most definitely not complaining.

On the other hand, time was beginning to drag in the office.

The first few weeks after star sling were filled with basic boot-up operations. Now the crew had settled back into its mundane rhythm, and everything felt numb. It was like everyone had lost a step. The mission was done—the real mission, anyway. The tension they had once had, or at least the sense of purpose that the mission once carried, was gone, leaving behind the fact that *Everguard* was a drifting relic now, a dinosaur on a mission that probably had an end game that included a good mothballing as a museum piece.

As far as Interstellar Command was concerned, *Everguard* was obsolete.

So, what did that say about her crew?

He grimaced and took a final swig of coffee, trying to bootstrap his energy for looking into issue number nine.

It was a lighting system problem, which he had pulled aside specifically because it seemed unusual.

He scanned the code calibration for D Deck and saw someone had reset the system to toggle the lights off through a different controller.

It was a prank.

Of course it was.

How many lieutenant commanders does it take to change a light bulb?

"Adjust the light node in compartment D112 to the on position, please, and reconnect the controllers to their standard configuration."

"Modification made."

"I need the service record for the last change made to this parameter."

"Light node D112 was last changed by Thomas Kitchell, identification key on screen."

Kitchell. Why didn't *that* surprise him?

The kid was the son of Indego Kitchell, the Nutrition Processing System director. He was fifteen, which meant he had been aboard for almost as far back as his memory could take him. The boy thought he was pretty sharp. And, Torrance had to admit, Kitchell *was* quick for his age—just not as bright as he thought he was. His brash approach to everything meant he was something of a punk, though, and his constant fiddling with the ship's basic wiring was a pain in the butt.

Looking at the tracking system, it was also clear that the kid had no idea what it meant to live on a ship that could track every movement you made.

Torrance had more than half a mind to go down to Education Deck and give the kid hell, except that he had too much to do already.

He had to submit the duty roster, then provide budgetary estimates to Romanov. Developmental plans for each of his people were due tomorrow, system availability metrics the day after that. Security Officer Casey would get his standard access reports at the end of the week—a step that made Torrance nervous despite his confidence in the system.

They would do it all again two standard weeks later, creating a whole new set of administrative vapor work that also meant nothing.

Joy of all joys.

He focused on the grunt work, but his brain turned all sorts of mental acrobatics to keep him from making progress. His fingers didn't want to move the toggles that would set the roster. His brain refused to think about the staff. His eyes kept drifting to some random movement outside his office.

Finally he gave in and stepped back.

All he wanted to do was see Marisa and dig into the Eden files, but it was too early—for both.

He had found a sweet zone right at the end of his shift when it was quiet enough that he could work with the Eden data here in his office. If he was cautious, and if he kept it to himself, he could pipe into several of the more powerful data parsing routines that came from the Signal Processing Lab. He had all the system codes, and he could cover his tracers. No one else had to know.

The idea of the pod crashing into Eden's surface came over him again.

It made him bittersweet, made him think about the world as even bigger than anyone else knew it was.

He imagined creatures approaching the pod as it lay crumpled.

They would be bipedal with long arms and weird, elongated legs. Science fiction come to life.

He laughed at himself when he recognized the creatures as a memory of an adventure game he used to play as a kid. Fat chance that aliens would ever look like something some programmer who probably worked in some tiny sweatshop of a compartment had dreamed up.

As if on autopilot, Torrance accessed his private space and pulled up the data from Eden.

He ran a frequency plot.

The data fell apart in the midrange, but was more firm in the lower frequencies. The power density of the waves was remarkably strong and intensely chaotic, a characteristic that probably led the analyst program to classify the event as a storm.

But the data varied considerably from pass to pass.

He cut it into different meta-categories and stored them off for later.

The signal's curves clung to him.

He sensed a pattern here that was almost there in the periphery of the power spectrum, but not quite. It was like a thought in a lucid dream, a piece of information that slipped away as soon as he turned directly toward it.

He peered into the depth of the holo-pad, feeling the data as if it was a real thing, as if the vibration of the signals rubbed up against his skin.

It was, he would have said if someone had asked him then, as if the data was actually whispering to him.

Torrance checked the time and nearly panicked.

A half hour had passed.

He glanced out the clear panes of his office. No one had seen him.

He released the information from his projector, cleared the path logs that would let anyone trace his steps, and stepped away from his screen.

That was dumb, he thought. He had to be more careful.

Certain he was safe now, however, he found his thoughts were still deep enough into the data that coming back to the real world was like pulling his head out of quick sand.

The ideas he was immersed in clung to him with annoying persistence.

In general, working on personal projects while on duty would be fine. Torrance was well known for blurring shifts—meaning he was essentially on call at all times, so his personal and work life were never separated by much more than a page. But if anyone understood what he was doing, and if that news were to leak …

He stretched his neck and pictured Security Officer Casey standing over him.

Torrance needed to study this, though.

He really couldn't ignore it.

Sitting alone in his office, the need to know what was going on burned throughout his entire body with power that was as physical as his need for Marisa.

The afterglow of his run through Eden's data felt so similar it was embarrassing.

He glanced out his office at the status boards.

Each of the crew was at their stations, except for the artificial gravity team, which had left to deal with an issue at the physical fitness command. Their status symbol flashed yellow on the board.

Torrance turned back to his own workstation.

The duty roster peeked out from the edge of his glass-top display.

He had work to do, budgets to budget, toilet systems to toilet.

Joy.

RON COLLINS

Welcome to my life.

Chapter 16

UGIS *Everguard*
Ship Local Date: June 13, 2204
Ship Local Time: 0913

The next day's incident report described the situation well enough that Torrance didn't have to check it out in person to understand the details. A maintenance bot had somehow gotten into the ductwork, made it down to D Deck, and used a paint sprayer to cover much, if not all, of a young man's sleeping quarters in red tomato paste.

It could have been only Thomas Kitchell.

Enough.

Torrance stomped through Systems Command with his brow furrowed and his jaw set. Young Thomas had hacked his last piece of code. The kid was going to be killed, that was all there was to it.

He tried Kitchell's personal quarters, then the holo-game area.

He tried Education Deck, then the mess.

He even tried the low-g tumbling center.

He finally found Kitchell in the Technical Library, a room about the size of a decent restaurant back home on Earth, with tables and data projectors spaced out to facilitate comfortable use.

It felt strange to see the kid sitting here with his back to the door, studying a lesson cube about optical spectrum transistors. He was small for his age. Dirty blond hair just a bit long and equally unkempt fell toward shoulder blades that stuck out from his blue shirt like the rims of coat hangers. Torrance had always felt at home in the Tech Library, like this was his place. Yet the essence of Kitchell's presence here, and the way he seemed to have taken over the system he was at gave Torrance an off sense of territorial discomfort.

He didn't like someone in his space.

"Mr. Kitchell?" Torrance said.

Kitchell craned his neck to look up.

Red stereo buttons filled his ears. The circles under his eyes were shiny with oil.

No pimples yet, Torrance thought. Just give him time.

"What's the matter?" Kitchell nearly shouted.

"Take the music out, Mr. Kitchell."

Kitchell picked a button out of one ear and gave him a stare that suggested Torrance was beyond rude and may well be interrupting something on the scale of a universe-wide peace conference.

"Can I help you?" the boy said.

"What can you tell me about Robert Frazier's sleeping quarters, Mr. Kitchell?"

"I don't know nothing about Robert Frazier's sleeping quarters," Kitchell said. "Except that it can't possibly get used for anything but a good fist-pounding every night, if you know what I mean."

Torrance merely maintained his stare.

"I can tell you Frazier's a dick."

"I appreciate your opinion, but I don't think that has anything to do with my question."

"What are you picking on me for? He's the one who started it."

"I don't care what occurred between you and Robert Frazier, Mr. Kitchell. But I do care what you do with my ship. I will not let you use our ventilation ducts and our robots to attack a crewmate."

"I don't know what you're talking about."

"Don't give me that crap. I am beyond tired of cleaning up after your escapades. So this time, you're the one who's going to do it."

"Do what?" The kid glared.

Torrance raised a pointed finger. "You are going to grab a mop and a bucket, and you are going to clean the wall and the floor of Robert Frazier's quarters. Then you are going to do his laundry.

After that, you are going to disassemble the ventilation grating, and clean that area of the ductwork to ensure we don't get tomato sauce decomposing on my ship."

"Bullshit."

Torrance bent down and got in Kitchell's face.

"You want bullshit? I'll tell you about bullshit. Bullshit is trying to run an entire ship's systems when you've got a dumb-assed kid tinkering around like he knows what the hell he's doing. Bullshit is wasting an hour and a half trying to find that dumb-assed kid. And bullshit is listening to that same dumb-assed kid tell me I'm wrong when I've got his identification code captured as accessing almost every system I control."

"Wha—"

"That's right, Mr. Kitchell. I can track every movement you make. I've seen every line of code you've ever touched. And, to take it a step further, I've been programming since before you were born. If you ask me, you're not as hot as you think you are."

The kid turned all sorts of dark colors.

Torrance continued.

"So, either you do what I tell you to do, or you suffer a formal reporting of this to your parents and to the psych officer."

Kitchell stammered.

The threat to his parents wouldn't faze the kid, but if Torrance knew Kitchell's profile at all, he knew the idea of a trip to the psychologist had him flummoxed.

"Your choice," he said. "But make it now."

The kid shut his mouth. His gaze flickered sideways as the room around them settled into a tone of stunned silence.

"I'm not doing his laundry."

Torrance didn't respond.

"Frazier will tell my Mom and Dad, anyway."

"Are six months with Dr. Taylor worth it?" Torrance finally said, watching with no little degree of satisfaction as the question settled.

"All right," Kitchell finally said. "Show me where the mop is."

CHAPTER 17

It was later that evening before Torrance could manage to laugh, but when the time came, it was all he could do to keep a straight face.

He and Marisa were lying in bed, Torrance on his back.

She had not moved in so much as they had just come to the point where she slept in his quarters because it was more comfortable for her. Fewer people to deal with, she told him. Less time needed to get ready in the morning.

It totally worked for him.

Of course, Torrance would have been happy with pretty much anything that resulted in her staying. Sure, it was a little strange to have someone in his room again. It had been years since the divorce. And, yes, military and standard-oriented or not, Marisa had her own way on things. But he didn't care. Need a place with more space? Bingo. Pull the sheets off the bed, isn't that cute. Prefer my toothpaste? I'll go down to the PX and get more.

As they lay there that night, the compartment was dark, with only the barest of light coming from the safety system. The weight of the bedclothes fell over his skin, and soft heat of Marisa's body was a presence beside him when, all of a sudden, Torrance was giggling uncontrollably.

"What?" Marisa said, rolling over and putting her arm around his waist. Her features were dim, but he could pick them out. Her eyes glittered with the blue component of the light.

"Oh," he said. "It's that kid. Kitchell."

He couldn't tell if her sigh was one of exasperation or humor. Humor, he hoped.

"What about him?" she said.

He described their discussion.

"You should have seen the expression on his face when I said I would send him to psych."

"You're a bad man, Mr. Black."

"Yes, I suppose I am." Torrance got a smug grin. "Felt good though."

"Mmmmm. I suppose it did."

They lay like that for a while.

"Tell me about your ex-wife," Marisa said.

Torrance sighed. "So much for feeling good, huh?"

"Is it that bad?"

The sheets ruffled as Torrance sat up in the darkness and crossed his legs. He set the temperature cool at night, and the air chilled his back. He figured this discussion was coming sooner or later.

She sat up beside him and ran her hand over her hair in a way that was already familiar to him.

"No. Not really. Adrienne was great, actually. We met while I was at the Academy. Everything was good for a while, but things change, you know? We split up a couple months before the *Everguard* slot came along."

"What changed?"

He shrugged. "Mostly kids, I guess. Adrienne wanted kids."

"And you didn't?"

"We tried." Torrance pursed his lips. "But it turns out I can't be a father."

There it was, the so-called pregnant pause.

"Oh. I'm, uh, sorry to hear that."

"It's all right. Just another thing I can't do."

"Don't talk like that. There are other ways, you know? Clone. Adopt."

"Yeah, believe me, I know."

"But?"

He shook his head. "I don't know. I just couldn't bring myself to get comfortable with the idea."

"But—"

"I know." Torrance raised his hand. "I know. We even talked about DNA grafting and a few other more eccentric ideas. I just couldn't do it…I just couldn't get over the idea that every time I looked into the kid's face, I would be reminded of my own failure."

"Sounds to me like you were just scared."

"And embarrassed. Don't forget embarrassed."

"Do you still feel the same way?"

"I don't know."

The question bothered him.

"You want to start a family?" he finally said.

"No," Marisa said more vehemently than Torrance had expected. "I'm not exactly a homemaking kind of girl, you know?"

"That's what I figured," he said. "You're clearly all service."

"That's not a problem, is it?" she asked.

"No. Not a problem at all."

They were quiet again.

"You know what I think?" Marisa said.

"What do you think?"

"I think you should talk to the kid again."

"Kitchell?"

"Yeah. See if he wants to be a techie. If he does, then you could mentor him."

"Ah, be a surrogate dad."

"More like an uncle."

"Kitchell needs a lobotomy more than he needs an uncle."

She ran her hand over his back.

"Don't sell yourself short, LC. If the kid is excited about shipboard systems, he needs someone who is just as excited about them to teach him."

"And I'm just the guy, eh?"

"No one else on board gets tears in their eyes when they talk about garbage processing equipment."

Torrance chuckled.

"It could be good for you. It would look good on the record when we get home. Besides," she said, bringing a mocking lilt to her voice, "it beats spending all your time thinking about life on Eden."

Torrance froze. He hadn't talked to her about the Eden files, because he didn't know how she would feel about him ignoring a direct order and perhaps even doing a bit more than breaking a law. She was, as he said, all service. He didn't think she would see this situation quite the same way he did, so at this point he figured it was better to let sleeping navigation officers lie.

"How...?" He stopped. "Silvio."

"He's never been one to keep a story close to the chest."

He frowned. "Shit. What did he say?"

"It's not a big deal, Torrance."

"What did he say?"

She rolled over onto her back. "Just that the two of you were studying the data files together before the launch, and that at one point you thought they might be aliens calling out for pizza."

He dropped his head.

"Who else has he told?"

"Everyone, I guess. You know how these things go. But it's really not a big deal. I don't think anyone really thinks much of it. Pizza delivery is funny, you know? You could lighten up a bit more."

Torrance let the comment settle. It was going to be all right. Silvio had just told the pizza story. She didn't actually know he had the data files.

"Great. So now I'm a laughingstock."

"That's okay, though." She lay back on the bed. "I think it's kind of cute."

He took a breath and tried to relax.

She was right. He could lighten up a bit more, he supposed.

His first concern, obviously, was that Silvio had actually caught him in the files themselves, but that wasn't the case. As long as everyone was talking about just pizza he doubted Casey would tie the two together. So he could live with it. It worried him, though. He didn't like investing whatever was left of his career into the idea that the ship's government security officer would miss that detail, as semi-small as it might seem.

"You want to know what I think?" he said, turning back to Marisa.

Her face was outlined in the darkness. He propped his head with one hand and ran the other over the smooth skin of her belly.

"I think you are about the most beautiful woman in the universe."

Marisa laughed out loud and tried to twist from his grasp.

Torrance grabbed on, held tight, and kissed her.

She giggled again and reached for him. "I suppose you say that to all the lieutenants?"

"Only the ones where it's actually true."

A moment later he knew he was in for another rough morning.

Such are the penalties for being bold.

Chapter 18

UGIS *Everguard*
Ship Local Date: June 18, 2204
Ship Local Time: 1015

As he strode through the nearly empty hallway toward Education Deck, Torrance enjoyed the fresh tingle of excitement that picked at his sense of calm. He was usually a little more pragmatic than aspirational, but today he enjoyed the idea that he was doing something special. The fact that it was all Marisa's fault just made him that much happier.

The flooring absorbed his footsteps in such a way as they disappeared into the background. The walls were two-toned, the lower half a faded blue, the upper half an off-white that made it less sterile than it might otherwise be. The upper panels were covered with images the students had put there as part of history class.

The image of a wormhole pod falling into a star caught his eye.

Sure, dropping the wormhole pods into the center of Alpha Centauri was an interesting legacy, but it was something anyone could have done if given the role.

But changing a kid's life was different.

Work with a kid, and you change the kid, Marisa had said at breakfast earlier in the day. *Change the kid, and from that day forward everything they do has a line back to you.*

He liked that.

The idea of mentoring Kitchell had been tugging at him ever since Marisa suggested he take the kid under wing, and the more he thought about it the more attractive the idea had become. The idea made him feel bigger. Marisa had helped him see that helping Kitchell would give him a touch of that very odd sense of immortality that people talked about when they discussed their children, and that so many people seemed to depend on in some way or another.

Who would have known he was one of them?

He came to the classroom.

The doorway was closed, but the low white noise of conversation radiated from it.

He peered through the glass.

The room was done in an open plan, full of teenaged kids who milled about in whatever haphazard situation they felt comfortable with. Some stood around a computer table, others lay on cushioned chairs, reading or marking on scribble plates. The team of instructors huddled together at the back of the room, talking about something in animated tones.

Now that he was here, a burst of nervous tension pressed against the back of his neck.

"Get your act together," he muttered. "Kitchell's just a kid."

He stood taller and settled himself down.

He could talk to kids. Hell, he'd just finished handing Kitchell a punishment. But this was different, and he knew it. As soon as Torrance stepped into this room, he was making a personal commitment about something outside his ability to completely control.

He pressed the door mechanism and stepped into the room.

All activity continued as if he wasn't there.

"Lieutenant Commander," one of the instructors said as he picked his way through the students. "How excellent to see you here. What can we do for you?"

"Can I speak to Thomas Kitchell?"

The room grew palpably quiet.

"He's over there," the instructor said.

The young man pushed back from a lab table.

Torrance walked through the room, aware of how his green and blue Systems Command jacket, even worn in the informal unsealed fashion, set him apart him from these kids who parted before him like water before Moses. Their movement gave him a sense of control as he drew close to Kitchell.

A circuit card with a tangled mass of wires and components sat on the gray table in front of the young man. An alkaline battery sat beside the assembly, but wasn't connected.

Kitchell seemed to have grown an inch in the few days since Torrance last saw him. A blotch of acne grew high up on his cheek.

"Old-school electrical assembly," Torrance said with a smile. "I love the basics."

"I didn't do nothing," Kitchell said, squinting as he looked up from his chair.

"I didn't say you had."

"What do you want, then?"

Torrance peered at the mess of wires on the table.

"What are you working on there? Ah—an oscillating circuit. Depending on what you're planning to time, you would be better served to use a purified ceramic crystal."

The kid held his tongue.

Torrance sat beside Kitchell and pushed wiring around on the circuit board. The kid's loops were too big, not a problem in a school lab, but potentially faulty in critical ship systems where sudden electromagnetic shifts can play havoc with sensitive electronic systems.

"You're pretty good with these things," Torrance said. "And I know you've got a lot of, uh, energy for playing with equipment."

Kitchell's blue-green eyes narrowed.

"How would you like to work on shipboard systems?"

"What?"

"You would work directly for me—mostly grunt work at first, replacing black boxes and running diagnostics, but as you get more familiar with the layout of the ship, I could see you getting deeper into testing and troubleshooting. If you do your job well you could get into some pretty slick stuff."

"What's your angle?"

"No angle at all."

"I don't need no grunt work."

"Don't run down grunt work. It's how you learn the guts of a system." Torrance sat back in his chair and picked at his jacket arm, then took the kid in. "That's what you're about, isn't it? Understanding the way things work?"

"Damn right."

"A good sensor. A software routine that runs faster than another one. They're gorgeous, aren't they?"

"They're truth," Kitchell said, while the widening of his eyes exposed the rabid sense of youth that bubbled in his gaze.

Torrance smiled. "I've got no angle here, Mr. Kitchell. If you're interested, I'll help you work on systems as you're ready for them. If you're not interested, then I'll go away and mind my own business."

Kitchell peered at him.

"There is one catch."

The kid got an "I told you so" expression.

"I find you messing with restricted systems again without my authorization, you're gone. No warning, no appeals, no nothing."

Kitchell pushed his bangs off his face and looked at his oscillator circuit. "You'll let me work on real systems?"

"That's what I'm offering."

"That's edge," he said.

"Edge?"

"You know. Good. Cool. Phreak. Whatever."

"So you'll do it?"

"When can I start?"

"I need some approvals to make everything legit, but how about you show up at my office after your classes today and we'll talk about what gets you excited."

"That's a deal." The kid held out his bony hand.

Torrance shook it, then stood, finally noticing that every face in the room had been watching them.

"Have a good day," he said to them all, then stepped toward the door.

The young man next to Kitchell elbowed him as Torrance left. "That's edge ..."

"So goddamned edge it's bleeding," Kitchell replied quietly.

The door shut behind Torrance.

He grinned to himself.

The kids were right. That *was* pretty edge.

Mid Flight

Chapter 19

UGIS *Everguard*
Ship Local Date: June 18, 2204
Ship Local Time: 1815

Marisa had a team social to attend that night, so after the kid left his office, Torrance took advantage of the quiet of late-shift to pull the data files. It was a glorious way to cap off the day, a full evening set aside to focus on the files from the safety of his office. It was still dangerous, of course. He would have to be careful. But he knew how to be careful, and the idea of being alone in the Command gave him what may have been the tiniest bit of a bloated sense of control and oversight, which he could admit to himself felt good.

He liked when things were in control.

And he liked working in binges, focusing in longer spans that brought on that hazy zone where it was like he was swimming in data.

He picked at the file, mapping the evening's analytical steps the way an archaeologist might make a grid on an open dig site. It was a game for him, his own little puzzle. How quickly could he prepare the parsing routines? How much sophistication could he put into the reporting tools he was developing? How much of the pattern recognition routine could he run in private channels in the background?

He accessed the central signal processing libraries with his ghost admin account, and picked out some custom analyzers he had found in the private spaces of three sharp engineers—Silvio Nivead expressly being one of them—carefully removing every trace of his actions. He ran the waveform from the Eden disturbance through the analyzers, hoping he could find a stable shape that would give him something he could then cut even further. He filtered frequencies. He ran interference patterns, did fractal transformations, and put them through higher ordered filters.

When each day's segment was complete, he recorded the findings—or lack thereof.

There were no matches in the linguistic database.

No stability to the waveform.

Nada. Squat. Bupkis.

And that added up to say he was probably wrong about life on Eden. Or, more likely, he just didn't have the mathematics background to figure it out on his own.

He didn't like either of those ideas.

Suddenly the ship clock somehow said it was 2220 hours. The realization made him hungry.

Torrance put his toys away, cleaning his pathway as he did so. No mistakes, he thought. He had to be meticulous. No paths to give him away.

"Abke," he said when he was done. "Patch me through to Marisa Harthing."

"Hey," her voice came through his speaker. "What's up?"

"I know you're probably getting ready for bed, but I wondered if you wanted to join me for a midnight snack at the observation mess."

"What?" she replied in false monotone. "And just watch the stars together?"

"I can only think of one other thing that's better," he replied.

Even though he couldn't see her, he could feel her smile. He had never felt this comfortable with someone before.

"Sounds delish."

"Ten minutes?"

"I'll be there."

He shut the link and left the office.

Yes, life was good.
Very good.

Chapter 20

UGIS *Everguard*
Ship Local Date: January 13, 2205
Ship Local Time: 0722

Torrance stood in Systems Command, taking in the main status panel and feeling the weight of everyday work pressing in on him. It was going to be a busy day. On top of all the routine stuff, C Deck was reporting an issue with their hydraulic lifter, and the control panel showed that the laundry bot hadn't been updated as planned. He had to follow up with Yarrow about that. Or maybe give it to Kitchell.

The boy was good—a hell of a lot better than Torrance thought he would be. He was energetic, and active.

And he was good on the deck, too. The team liked having someone around who could ask the obvious dumb question that often turned out to not be so dumb after all. Torrance had to face the fact that the kid's brash act was really just that—a defense mechanism made necessary because he was quicker than the kids around him, and quicker than most of the adults around him, too.

His standard response to any challenge was *"Hey, take a chance, right?"*

Sure, there were times Torrance would prefer the kid was a little less daring. The day Kitchell screwed up and had to reset the entire power feed for the Rearward janitorial bots would be legend among Systems Command for the rest of the trip, but Torrance had come to realize that half the time he wasn't taking a chance at all—that half the time, Thomas Kitchell knew what the answer was, and that he was just buffering the situation for the idiots around him who didn't understand the system.

Of course, the other 50 percent he was actually taking a chance.

Either way, the fact was that Torrance liked working with Thomas Kitchell, and he figured the kid could probably handle this one as it was. Maybe it would be a good one to let him run solo on.

But none of that was very interesting right now.

His brain was loaded with a question.

An idea.

A flame of thought about his latest run through the Eden files had been rattling though his brain all morning, screwing with his thoughts so hard that Marisa had tossed a fit at him for not listening as she ran through her day's calendar. It had grabbed hold of his mind so firmly that he couldn't concentrate on anything else long enough to be productive.

The game was afoot, as it were.

He was wondering if he could split the signal and triangulate multiple positions—that perhaps the signal wasn't actually a single entity, but had been created from different sources, two or three or even more, and that those sources had somehow interfered with each other.

He wanted to know if his theory was possible, but the start of the day was closing in on him.

"Are you okay?"

It was Yarrow. She was bright-faced and ready for the day. Like always.

"Yes, thank you," Torrance replied. "If you see Kitchell, tell him to come to my post, will you?"

"He'll be a little later, I think. He has a test at 0800."

"That's fine," Torrance replied, thinking that it would give him time alone.

He went to his office and commanded the glass panel door to close behind him. "Projector on," he said. "View to back." He walked around his desk, and his gaze made a last pass at the nearly empty command floor. He had ten, maybe twenty minutes.

It wouldn't take him long.

He had to know.

"Abke," he said. "Please access my personal space."

"Accessed."

He cut a stream from the first flare and ran a quick Fourier transformation, then pushed it through a matcher, looking through the map for multiple mathematical patterns. He parsed frequencies and created a multidimensional model based on what they knew of the planet's geography in the area—which was a fascinating study on its own, an area dominated by a single curved ridge of mountainous rock. Then he set the system to run on a pattern that moved two, then three hypothetical transmitters around on the ground, trying to find combinations that might make the signature.

Graph theory on amplifiers, he thought.

Nothing.

He picked another waveform at random.

Still nothing.

Maybe he would try a broader spread between the transmitters.

He kneaded away the headache that was beginning to grow. He had a lot more work to do on this idea.

"You have a call from the captain," Abke said in its base monotone.

Torrance snapped back to attention.

Damn it!

He looked at the clock and ran his hand through his hair, shaking some life into his arms. Fifteen minutes had flown.

"I'll be right there."

Each morning, after his yoga and before his morning fruit cup, Alexandir Romanov reviewed security reports generated the night before. The reports were complete and concise, a running list of each offense against standard code of conduct by each member of the crew.

They were all upsetting, of course.

Neural scientists could talk about body chemistry, dopamine reaction patterns, and synaptic pathway channels until they were out of breath. Free will, they said, wasn't so free. People were a slave to their brain chemistry.

But Romanov saw these things as simple: know the rules, follow the rules.

He didn't understand why people did things they shouldn't be doing.

But one name on his list bothered him beyond all others.

The door chime rang as he stared at the name.

"Lieutenant Commander Black, sir," Abke said.

Romanov sat back.

"Let him in, please."

The door slid open.

Torrance stepped into the captain's office.

It was crisp and clean, much like Torrance remembered Romanov's personal quarters, but more so. Dark blue carpet spanned the floor. The walls were coated with full-scale active slate that would allow any portion to be used as a projection device. Most panels were dark now, but three held feeds with reports from Romanov's direct staff. Torrance wondered if the captain had left Kip Levitt's status memo on the wall closest to him on purpose or if that was a fluke of random luck.

"Please have a seat," Romanov said tersely.

"Good morning, sir," Torrance said as he followed Romanov's command.

The captain glanced at his screen, then back to Torrance. He wore ship fatigues and the gaunt look that spoke of limited sleep. Everyone assumed the return flight would be a piece of cake, and it should be. But it was still a big piece of cake, and despite the quips of several crew members, Romanov was as human as the next guy. For a moment, Torrance wondered if the flight back was more than the captain could handle.

When Romanov remained silent, a gangly sense of unease crawled up Torrance's back. A film of sweat moistened his palms, so he rubbed them on his pant legs. The room smelled dangerous.

"What can I do for you, sir?"

"I have been looking at your performance."

"Yes, sir."

"I know in the past we had discussed…possibilities."

"Yes."

"I doubt very seriously whether this can happen."

"I don't understand."

"As I'm sure you are aware, the fleet has been building several new ships, all of them Star Drives with young crews performing extravagant feats. Given the speed of transmission, I suspect that we'll begin receiving updates on them in a year or so."

"I'm sure we will, sir." Torrance wondered where this was going. "What's wrong with my performance?"

"Technically," Romanov said. "It has been spotless."

Torrance waited.

"However," Romanov said. "The performance of a lieutenant commander who is not on a Star Drive has to be better than technically spotless in order to be considered for advancement. This is especially true given the competition that will await such a lieutenant commander."

"Yes, sir."

"So, you see why I suggest I will be unable to promote you."

"No, sir. I can't say that I see anything, yet."

"Mostly it has to do with data files."

Torrance felt ice grow in his chest.

"Data files, sir?"

The captain's gaze was so sharp Torrance could imagine curled talons. "Display Report C, masked," he said to the system while keeping his gaze on Torrance. A panel flickered with a new report, all line items but one blacked out. That one read: *Black, Torrance – ZA1252, SLT 2158,76543, SLD 22050111, Sector D-12*. It was, Torrance realized, an access report that had picked up something he had missed in his cleanup.

The ice in his chest turned to a ball of fire.

Romanov knew.

"Was I not clear in my directions?" Romanov said. "Did you not understand that you were to drop the issue of life on Eden?"

"Yes, sir. I understood."

"And still you have pulled data from classified memory space."

Torrance remained silent.

He didn't know exactly what to be mad about—Eden, himself, or Romanov—so he let them all jumble together in one simmering mass. He had screwed up somewhere. He had all the base files in his own system, but occasionally still had to access certain tools and applications from other places. Somewhere along the line he had forgotten to mod an access log, or been overseen somehow.

Totally stupid.

"I'm not sure what to say, sir," Torrance replied.

"I think truth is the best option," said Romanov.

Torrance's defenses rose, and in a flash he also realized a weakness in Romanov. The captain wasn't certain what he was dealing with. And kept secrets can cut both ways. While it was true that Torrance had been hiding his work, it might be equally true that Romanov had been hiding it, also. The idea left him stunned for a moment. He understood the game he had to play now, but he wasn't certain he was…bold…enough to play it.

The question at hand now was to discover if Romanov was pulling a standard security report, in which case Security Officer Casey would also be aware of it, or if he was doing his own sleuthing.

"I've not lied to you, sir," Torrance said, gripping the arms on his chair.

Romanov gave a gruff snort.

"I'm not talking about today, Lieutenant Commander, and you know it. You haven't actually answered my question. So, I ask again: do you deny having pulled data from secure storage?"

"I have no comment on it either way, sir."

Romanov pursed his lips.

"I see."

"Hypothetically, though," Torrance said. His heart pounded, but the words came out sounding almost confident. "I think it might be an unhappy case for both of us if it ever came to light that such a thing had actually happened."

The captain put his fingers together and regarded Torrance with a new fire in his eyes.

"Be very careful, Lieutenant Commander. I can absorb more than you think I can."

That was all Torrance needed.

Romanov was working on his own here. Casey was in the dark.

"I'm being as careful as I can be, sir. And I wouldn't want you to have to absorb anything you didn't have to. We both know how tenuous long and successful careers can be."

"Very diplomatic today, aren't we?"

Torrance didn't respond, so Romanov continued.

"I agree with your overall assessment, though."

The captain sat upright and put his hands together before him, elbows on the table. A wave of his aftershave rolled over Torrance.

"And I agree that the record of your relatively harmless dalliance should be kept off the record. I also think, however, that you can see why I say it is still unlikely that you will be seeing a full promotion anytime in the near future."

"Yes, sir, I can see reasons for both of those comments."

"I also need to tell you that while the specifics of this insubordination will stay off the record, I am considering a formal reprimand for your handling of access codes."

Torrance clenched his teeth. "I was only—"

"You were only looking for life on Eden. Something that you and I both agreed we would not do. I will play your game, Torrance, because I know your lack of self-control is not putting the mission at risk, and because it is the wisest thing for me to do. I will not, however, be lied to and then held for ransom without providing some form of repercussion." The captain paused. "I was not lying, either, when I said I can absorb more than you think."

Torrance swallowed and tried to come up with a reasonable response before finally settling on the truth.

"I didn't mean any harm, sir. I tried to keep it to myself."

"This is not a small issue, Torrance. You understand that, right? I went very far out on a ledge for you. I expect you will honor that. You are right that I would prefer it kept quiet, but you should understand that this only goes so far. If this crashes and burns, I promise you that I will come out of it well enough, whereas you…will be buried."

Torrance felt the stakes rise as Romanov called his raise and raised him back.

"And, if this ever happens again, Torrance, I'll have Security Officer Casey on your ass so fast he'll be gnawing on your spleen before you even know it's gone."

"I understand, sir."

Romanov sat back. His chest rose with a breath that he let out from his nose in one long stream.

"I have decided to refrain from formal reprimand," he said. "But your name is on a security record and I cannot let this go totally unremarked upon. So let me be clear that I *will* put a notice in your dossier, though its wording will be vague—for now. Rest assured that if I find you in restricted memory space again, I will not be so forgiving."

Torrance swallowed hard, hesitated as he parsed words carefully.

"I will never access that memory space again, sir."

Romanov pressed his lips together. "That is what I heard the last time."

"Is that all, sir?"

"Yes, Torrance. You can go."

Torrance stood and left.

Technically, he had not lied.

That's what Torrance told himself as he stomped through the corridors of Forward Deck, ignoring glances and comments from crew members who parted before him as plowed ahead. He wanted to punch the wall, but restrained himself. He had been an idiot, of course. Stupid as hell. But Romanov's threat was the last domino to fall, the last piece of shit to hit the ventilator.

He could live with never seeing another promotion.

He didn't care. The idea of rising in the ranks sucked platypus.

The realization was strange and invigorating at the same time.

It felt like freedom.

Life was too short for this crap.

But ignoring the files was just not going to happen.

He took a deep breath and began walking again, this time slowly, with his head down and his hands clasped behind his back. The controlled swing of his pace and the rhythm of his feet on the soft composite flooring calmed him. As he watched his footsteps, he thought about the artificial gravity system that made *Everguard* so easily inhabitable.

That had been a concept-shattering advance, hadn't it?

And all it had taken was one person to stick to her guns to make it happen.

Of course, the concept of creating artificial gravity by lassoing the atomic weak force had been developed by big science and commercialized by the UG's favorite conglomerate corporation, but it had sprung from the mind of Emily Michaude, a lone physicist who followed an unpopular idea about antigravity to its seemingly illogical conclusion. That was the way of science, wasn't it? The way of almost all things in life, really. Sometimes he thought he was just being romantic, but in reality it was right. Every big idea came from one person. The Star Drive concept itself was born of a thought experiment related to Einstein's and Hawking's work, but extended by a single person—in this case, as oddity would have it, a painter. Almost all ideas of merit, inventions and concepts and structures that actually change the lives of people, come from a single place and then spread.

He loved that idea.

As he thought about antigravity, and Star Drives, and wormhole pods, his anger subsided. His body swayed with his stride. His mind settled. And as his mind settled one thought kept coming to him.

He hadn't lied.

Romanov said to stay away from classified memory space.

Torrance had made that promise.

But that meant the old bastard didn't know that Torrance had saved the data to his personal system.

Torrance nodded to himself as he walked.

He needed to be alone. He needed to think this over.

Chapter 21

UGIS *Everguard*
Ship Local Date: January 13, 2205
Ship Local Time: 1033

Thirty minutes later Torrance sat alone in the open cafeteria, spooning his cup of cold coffee to stir up the sweetener. Stars glimmered against the constant blackness outside the observation window, and the sound of dishes clattered in the distance. Something about the contrast between the immensity of space and the clatter of dishes made him angry. A field of stars, he thought, should not be accompanied by KP duty.

The mess hall was open and cavernous, but a sense of claustrophobia still managed to press on him.

"Torrance?"

Marisa stood beside the booth, her own coffee cup in one hand, fingertips of the other resting on the back of the bench across from him.

"You look glum."

He raised his eyebrows and held back a grimace. He had no desire to speak, which made the silence between them awkward.

"Can I join you?"

"Sure."

"So much enthusiasm."

She slid into the seat and wrapped her long fingers around her cup as she cradled it before her.

"What's the matter?"

He gave a derisive laugh, trying to decide how much to tell her.

It was only fair that she know *something*. But how far should he go? How much could he say without giving her so much that the government security officer, or anyone else for that matter, could use her to piece together a story that was closer to the whole truth?

"Romanov filed a notice against me," he said.

"Whoa."

He put the spoon down and left his coffee swirling.

"That's not fair," she said.

"Romanov can do anything he wants."

"Yeah, but coming down that hard on you isn't right."

When Torrance didn't say anything, a new expression crossed Marisa's face.

"What did you do?"

He choked down a swig of cold coffee as another delaying tactic.

"I pulled secure data without authorization."

"Ouch," Marisa replied. "What data?"

"I don't think you really need to know that, now, do you?"

She pursed her lips and put both hands around her mug. "No, I suppose that wouldn't be right. I'm sorry I asked."

He gave her a doubting expression.

"I am." She sipped her coffee. "That's harsh for Romanov, though."

He shrugged.

"A notice for a first offense is pretty hard-nosed."

"It's not a first offense."

She smiled again, cradling the coffee cup on the table in front of her, her fingertips running lightly over its lip.

"Knowing you like I already do, I'm sure you've been playing with a billion things no one else would even think to touch. But what I meant was that if he hadn't told you—"

"I know what you meant."

Torrance looked at her. She frowned. He gripped the cup hard enough to wonder if the composite might crack under compression. No, he thought, giving himself a caustic, mental laugh. The material might shatter in an instant under tension, but the bones of his hands would crumble before the cup would break in compression. Why was he like that? Thinking these trivial things in the middle of things that were so much more important?

He was such a dumbass.

"Romanov gave me the order a long time ago."

A pallor came over her face, and her stare became hard.

"That was dumb, then," she said.

The words were like a knife to the lungs.

"Tell me how you really think."

"A captain gives you a direct order, you have to follow it."

"I wasn't hurting anything."

"Like that matters?"

"You can leave anytime you want." The words were out of his mouth before he could stop them, but now that they were out, it felt good.

"Don't be an ass, Torrance. I'm just trying to help."

"Berating me for things you don't understand isn't what I would call helping."

"What is it you think I don't understand?"

He stopped. How could he possibly explain what she didn't understand? She would never understand what those files represented to him. How could she when he couldn't even say exactly what they meant to him?

Life, maybe? Truth?

Yes.

But it was more than that, too.

He looked at Marisa as she sat across from him with raw judgment on her gaze, and the idea of losing the data files brought him a wave of panic and despair that made his chest ache. Those files were personal. They were a moment where he had stood up for himself, a pinpoint in time where he alone had made a decision to do the right thing. His entire world was falling in on him today, and here was Marisa—the one person in the entire universe that he thought he might actually trust—and she was—

"Torrance." Marisa touched his arm.

He flung her hand away and slid out of the booth to tower over her.

She flinched back in the seat, and something inside him went nova.

"Those files are important," he said through teeth clenched so hard it hurt. "They mean something—I'm absolutely certain of it."

"I don't understand."

He put his hands on the table and stared down into her face.

"I did it. I opened the files and I worked with them."

"Well—"

"And if I did it, that means they were important enough to do it, all right?"

"I still don't unders—"

"Of course you don't understand!" He stood straighter and gestured wildly as he raged, yelling now. "You *can't* understand. But you *could* trust me anyway!"

"I do trust you."

He clenched his jaw.

"Not if you're telling me I'm wrong."

He turned to leave.

"They're just data files, Torrance."

His reaction happened on its own. He twisted back to her, his hand cocked with an open palm prepared to strike her.

Her expression froze.

And he stopped himself.

In time.

Barely in time.

Marisa's cheeks turned an embarrassed scarlet.

Torrance dropped his hand in shame. He had lost control. It had been only one instant, one horrible instant, but he had lost it.

"I'm sorry," he said. "I'm really—"

Rather than reply, she stood up and left.

Chapter 22

UGIS *Everguard*
Ship Local Date: January 13, 2205
Ship Local Time: 2307

It was late, nearing the end of second shift, and it had been a very long day.

Torrance felt the stares as he headed back to his quarters. Support crews were exchanging glances in the crossing time between shifts, people he recognized but didn't work with. Traffic was high. He was tired. His head hurt, and his brain felt waterlogged.

Which of them knew he had threatened Marisa? Who did he have to be ashamed around?

He knew the answer, though. People talked. Everyone could know. Every glance could be an indictment, every cautious nod an accusation. He had to be ashamed around everyone.

He rubbed his eyes.

If fatigue made him lightheaded, the idea of facing Marisa now made him deeply uncomfortable. He would have to apologize, of course. But he wasn't sure he would be able to do it right. He was blithering idiot, and she would be mad—naturally. And hurt. He felt her anger from hours away.

She hadn't stopped by in the afternoon like she usually did.

She hadn't returned his pages.

He didn't blame her for either of those things. But she also hadn't been at her station or in the ship's library like he had anticipated. He hadn't, in fact, seen her at all since their fight—which scared him in some elemental way that went all the way to the bone. It was like she was avoiding him.

When he came to his quarters, he paused outside the door to gather his thoughts.

His apology had better be a good one.

Then he pressed the security lock.

The door slid back with a rasping sound that was loud in the late-shift silence of the hall, revealing only darkness.

He frowned.

It wasn't so late that Marisa would be sleeping.

He pressed on a light.

The table was cluttered with printout of code from the heating system's control loop—another problem he had let slip over the past few days. His dirty glass from this morning sat on the utility counter he had left pulled from the wall. His shirt from last night lay wadded on the floor where he had left it.

The bed remained unmade.

Everything was still and silent.

Marisa wasn't here.

And her stuff was gone.

He found her in the mess just as she had found him some twelve hours earlier—sitting in a corner booth and nursing a coffee. A plate of half-eaten scrambled eggs, bell peppers, and rice sat in front of her.

The pavilion was nearly empty, which made sound echo.

Third-shifters worked in the kitchen amid the sounds of clattering trays and cups that were moving through the washing conveyor. Cleaning bots scoured the floor and gave the area an aroma of cleanser. As the screws of fate would have it, Security Officer Casey was standing alongside two other officers in front of the observation window. The coincidence crawled under his skin.

Marisa stared out the observation panel as Torrance approached. Her blue work jacket was zipped to her throat, and the corners of the collar jutted up to make severe points at her jawline. Her bloodless lips tightened into a thin line that would have been screaming if it had a voice.

"Go home," she said when he arrived.

"I'm sorry."

He slid into the bench across from her, feeling sadness leak from her.

"I didn't invite you to sit."

"I will leave in a minute if you want me to."

"What do you want me to say, Torrance?"

"I'm sorry. I don't know what happened to me, but I'm sorry. I want you to say you'll come back."

Marisa steeled herself. Her lips set in that matter-of-fact way that said her mind was made up. Her fingers wrapped around her cup like it was a life vest.

"My first boyfriend hit me, Torrance. I never told you that before, because…well…it never seemed to matter."

"I'm sorry," he said again.

"I can't be with you anymore."

"Yes, you can. I've never, ever done anything like that. I was embarrassed and angry. I can promise it will never happen again."

"I don't trust you. But it's more than that."

"What do you mean?"

"We want different things."

"I don't understand."

"Don't make me do all this by myself, Torrance."

"I honestly don't know what you mean."

She drank from her cup. "I like you. You're sweet, you know? And you're good at what you do. You're better than you think you are. Most men are the opposite—so full of themselves they don't see they're assholes, you know? So I like that."

He waited.

"I want a career, Torrance."

"So do I."

"No." She shook her head. "You don't."

The fact that the accusation didn't sting told him she was right, but he didn't know what to say.

"I've been in the command for a lot of years, Marisa."

"Don't pretend, Torrance. Maybe you wanted a career once, when you joined up, or whatever. But you don't even know what having a career means now. You think you want one, and sometimes you even act like it, but mostly you just want to know how things work—and when the two conflict, it's the 'figuring out how things work' side that wins."

Torrance reached to take her hand.

She pulled it away.

"I *want* this life, Torrance. I *need* it. And I'll do whatever I need to do to make it work."

"I can change, Marisa."

She laughed out loud. "You can't change who you are, Torrance."

"I can," he pleaded. "For you, I can."

She raised her hand and Torrance became quiet.

"Don't do it this way, Torrance. Please. Just don't."

He swallowed down his emotion. She was right. He knew she was.

"Okay," he finally said. "Okay."

She drank coffee and stared out into space beyond the observation dome.

He stood and left.

Chapter 23

UGIS *Everguard*
Ship Local Date: January 14, 2205
Ship Local Time: 1503

The next day was as hard as any Torrance could remember. The aura of Marisa's departure clung to him like a second skin, and he was certain he was catching sideways glances from everyone he ran into. It felt like he had an electric field built up around him. By 1500 the pressure got to be too much to bear, and he slipped into his office.

It was silent here.

Three boxes of broken-down equipment sat in the far corner. A gutted refrigeration assembly sat just outside the door. His computer display flashed cold notifications in green and blue, one buzzing in a low frequency that demanded attention. Outside, pulsing lights detailed the status of each system on the ship.

"Abke, please set my message service off-line," he said as he sat down heavily. "Leave a note that says I'm on a high-priority task, and will return calls as soon as practical."

"Note set."

"Thank you."

He put his hand to his throbbing temple and sat in silence as the ventilation system pushed a flow of cool air over him.

Maybe he would be better off just going to his quarters.

No, he thought, going to his quarters at this time of day wasn't his norm, so that might set off Romanov's sensors. The idea of being passively monitored had never really bothered him before, but now he shivered with the understanding that the ship could track the inherent electrical signature his body put out, and that his body heat and e-lint could be used to follow him almost anywhere. It made him feel defenseless.

Of course, he didn't know if Romanov was actually doing anything of the sort. Or Casey, for that matter. But the sense of paranoia that swept over him now made everything different. He felt weak.

They were less than a year into the return flight. How bad could this get?

The duty roster was flashing yellow.

Shit.

The refrigerant system on C Deck had been off-line for over an hour. He checked the status of the work ticket and saw Kitchell was on it.

He sat back, knowing it would be taken care of.

Kitchell had only been working with them for six months, but adding the kid to the team might have been the best thing Torrance had done all flight—outside of saving off the data files, anyway. Yes, Thomas Kitchell was a hard worker when assigned the right tasks and given enough instruction to be successful. And, yes, he may well prove to be brilliant. But he still needed approval to feel good about himself. Once Torrance hit on that knowledge, they had gotten along more than fine. The kid was going to be a damned fine engineer one day.

He didn't care about that, though.

Marisa was gone, and he had no career. If he had a set of displays showing his own personal status, he wondered what shade of red they would be flashing in. But, Torrance also knew that in darkness is sometimes opportunity. He couldn't pretend that he didn't feel a new sense of purpose tugging at the back of his mind, or at least a stronger one.

"LC?"

Torrance looked up to find Thomas Kitchell leaning into the office. "What is it?"

"Are you all right?" the kid said.

"Yeah, I'm just tired."

Kitchell shrugged as if that wasn't really an acceptable answer but he wasn't going to dig any deeper.

"What can I do for you, Thomas?"

"I wanted to tell you I got the Air Quality network up and running again. And I reprogrammed the filter purge cycle a little, so I thought you would want to…" He shrugged again. "You know…take a look."

"Okay. Yeah, good. I'll check it out before I leave."

"Thanks."

Kitchell got an expression Torrance had come to know as a grin, even though it had nothing to do with his lips.

"Thanks for hopping on the C Deck thing, too," Torrance said. "You saved my backside."

Kitchell gave an actual smile then. "No problem," he said.

Torrance waited.

The kid hesitated. His expression made Torrance think of a rookie cadet prepping for his first open air leap in survival school.

"What is it?" Torrance said.

"Can I ask you a question?"

"Sure. Have a seat?"

He motioned to an open chair, and Kitchell came in to take it.

"It might make you mad."

"Tell me more."

"I, uh, I saw Security Officer Casey poking around in here earlier today."

"Really?" He sat up. This was news, and not good news.

"I know he was talking to some people, and I was wondering who it was about." Kitchell squirmed in his seat, trying to get comfortable.

"Do you have any reason to be concerned?"

"No."

Torrance waited.

"Well…maybe." The kid's voice got faster, and rose as he spoke. "But I didn't mean to do anything bad, and I got out as soon as I thought something was screwed up."

"Go on."

"I was working in the system a couple nights ago, you know, looking at cals and checking out how the ship's backup power system kicks on—we should switch up the collectors, by the way, it's like they were coded by some idiot on pico-zone. Totally whacked, you know? Anyway, in the process I found some things there that maybe shouldn't be there."

Torrance gripped the end of his chair arm, hoping his concern didn't show otherwise.

"What were they?"

"I don't really know." Kitchell's face got red. "Honestly, I don't. Some data files. Things that looked like noise studies, or information traces. I saw a log of events, too, and a bunch of other stuff that had obviously been wiped. When I did a full scan for residuals, I saw someone with big-balls security clearance had gone in and erased a bunch of stuff in the access logs, too."

"You're worried that Casey was after you?"

"Wouldn't you be?"

Torrance smirked.

"I swear I didn't do anything," Kitchell said.

"I'm sure you didn't," Torrance said, as much to calm the kid as to say he believed him.

He looked at Kitchell and tried to decide how to react.

It was clear the boy had seen the data files, and that he understood how to identify the fact that someone had deleted traces of their work—but he obviously didn't understand that in this case that someone was Torrance himself. It had always been possible that someone could do a root atomic scan of the crystals and find evidence of his deletion, but only someone like Kitchell would have thought to do it.

"I'm impressed you knew how to do an atomic level scan."

"Just something I was playing with."

Torrance hesitated. "Abke," he said to the computer. "Please close the doorway."

The door slid shut with a finalistic whoosh.

Kitchell's face drained of blood.

"This puts me in a difficult position," Torrance said.

"I know I wasn't supposed to be in there, but I swear I didn't do anything. I'm telling you this, aren't I? I'm being honest. Please don't throw me out."

"That's not the problem I'm struggling with, Thomas."

"I don't understand."

Torrance nodded. "I know. That's my problem."

He hesitated. Kitchell didn't know who had done the work, but he knew about the files and knew about Torrance's cleanup process. That meant the kid was a loose end.

The fact that the government security officer was poking around Systems Command could be just coincidence, but he doubted it. Casey may well be a bureaucratic ass, but he was an effective one as far as bureaucratic asses go. Romanov was clearly working on his own, so Torrance figured the captain wouldn't have reported anything to Casey about their conversation—too much of a chance for Casey to discover Romanov's own shortcomings, and Torrance thought it was a safe bet that senior officers could be trusted to avoid exposing themselves to the scrutiny of government security officers unless there's no alternative. However, Casey would certainly have heard about his outburst with Marisa. He guessed that meant Casey was taking advantage of the moment to put some pressure on him.

"The way I see it here," Torrance said to Kitchell, "I can either give you the full scoop or I can shut you out totally. Either way, since I know you've seen them, I need to tell you that those data files are important. And I need you to promise me you'll be quiet about what you've found."

"That shit is yours?" Kitchell said, his eyes growing wide. "I thought—"

"Yes, you thought it was Casey's. I know. But, yes, that 'shit' is mine, and I need you to promise to keep your mouth shut about it."

"I will. I promise."

Torrance gave him an appraising stare.

"What is it?" Kitchell said.

"That's the hundred-billion-solar question, isn't it? And the problem here is that I know you well enough by now to know you're going to tell me you'll never get into that space again, and that you're going to mean it…only you won't be able to stay out of it because that's not how you're wired."

"That's not true," Kitchell said, though his gaze told Torrance it most certainly *was* true.

Torrance laughed.

"Kid, don't even pretend. You and I are so much alike in that department that we might as well be father and son. I know you'll promise to stay away, but then the questions will get to building up inside you, and your fingers will get itchy, and next thing you know you'll be in for just a quick look."

Kitchell actually nodded. "Yeah, I'm edge with your whole thing, I guess. I mean, I think I'm a lot like you there."

Torrance took in the moment. "Hey, take a chance, right?"

Kitchell gave an embarrassed grin.

"If *I* take a chance here and tell you everything, I know I can be fairly sure you won't go blabbing because even you will see what a huge ball of crap I'm exposing you to if people find out. My problem is that if I tell you the details, I put you in a potentially dangerous position."

"What if you don't?"

Torrance chewed his lip.

What if?

"Screw the problems," Kitchell said. "They were from the planet, weren't they? The files? They were from the launch?"

Torrance laughed.

The kid was already ahead of him. His eyes were lit up like new stars, and his posture said he was ready to go. Torrance had to make a decision. If he didn't bring Kitchell into the fold it would piss him off, and then who knew what could happen. But how far could he trust this kid who was so much like him, but who was also prone to youthful exuberance that could get them both in serious trouble?

"I want to know, man," Kitchell said. "If they're from the launch, it'll be edge."

"All right," he said, making his decision. "Abke, please access my system, file 1."

The ship clock read 1740 when they were finished.

Kitchell's mind had been blown, and his approach to Torrance had changed. Suddenly, he wasn't LC. Now he was sir, as in sharp *yes, sir*'s or *no, sir*'s. They worked their way through the story together, and through the "loss" of the last wormhole pod. Torrance showed him the emissions files and some of the studies he had done.

"Edge?" Torrance asked when they were finished.

"A lot more than edge," Kitchell replied.

"You see why we can't ever talk about this outside?"

"Yes, I do."

"You see why you can't access these files without my permission?"

"I see you'll need to clean up after me, yeah. But maybe you can give me a security code to do it on my own?"

Torrance gave the kid his own version of the "are you an idiot?" stare—the one he had learned from Kitchell to begin with.

"All right," Kitchell said, sitting back from the projector. "When can I get to work on them?"

"Let's meet for dinner tomorrow," Torrance said. "We can talk then."

The kid nodded, and looked at the time. "I'm going to log out, then, if that's all right? Mom's going to be mad that I'm late."

"Sure," Torrance said.

"Have a good second shift," Kitchell said. Then he was gone.

Alone again, Torrance took a deep breath and put his head in his hands. Had he done the right thing?

"Abke, can you play my personal audio file E-1?"

"File playing."

Torrance sat back and closed his eyes. The sound was a soft white noise with the occasional crack or blip. No one else would know it, of course, but it was the audio playback of the files he had converted from the Eden data.

They popped and hummed in an eerie form of techno-jazz that he was finding strangely comforting.

So what if he hadn't been able to figure much out from them, yet? Maybe his latest idea of splitting the frequency fields and triangulating locations wouldn't give him anything, either. But the files were still talking to him, and now he had a co-conspirator to bounce ideas off of.

He sat back in his chair and closed his eyes as the steady fuzz of 700 megahertz static beat a pattern across his heart.

CHAPTER 24

UGIS *Everguard*
Ship Local Date: January 23, 2205
Ship Local Time: 1145

He was trying to concentrate, but it was still useless.

Torrance was back at his station at Systems Command, staring at next week's duty roster. Call it brain freeze, or burnout, or pure laziness, it didn't matter. Nothing would come. Maybe it would never come.

His eyes were dry and his brain hurt.

He hadn't slept more than a couple hours of lucid grayness last night before giving up and wandering the halls until breakfast. Then he had come to the office and buried his head into the day— which in the past would have been enough for him to deal with whatever shit had happened around him, but now was just serving to make everything worse.

It was damned frustrating, every day becoming just like the last, his brain going haywire and nothing seeming to be going right. He had lost Marisa. All his playing with the data files was still resulting in a big fat zero. He had put Kitchell into danger, and was now struggling to keep up with the kid's interest—Kitchell nagged him for partial access to files every night, which was already getting annoying and it had only been a week or two since the kid had "joined the team."

And now he couldn't work.

He felt…adrift.

Had he lost it?

Even the idea of working in the Eden files was mind-numbing.

He focused hard on the work roster.

Two crew members had asked for slots in second shift, and another had been sick for three days, which made the overtime roster swell, which brought the finance folks down on him like a bunch of angry sharks.

Once the duty roster was filled out, Torrance still had to run status reports on every repair system on the ship and compile the routine system-availability metric.

Crap. His brain would not focus.

Abke interrupted.

"Message, sir."

Torrance straightened. The fact that he wasn't progressing made the interruption just that much more aggravating.

He wanted to be alone.

"Put it through, please."

It was Lieutenant Malloy.

"Yes, Karl?"

"Are you okay, sir?"

"I'm fine. Why?"

"Nothing, sir."

Malloy didn't have to say anything. Torrance knew his response had been too sharp.

"I apologize," he said.

"No problem. Up for a round on the range?"

Torrance looked at the duty roster.

"I can't spare the time."

"Come on, boss. You're spending all your time holed up in that office of yours."

"Really? I hadn't noticed."

"You're not as dense as you try to put on, LC. You've got to get out and have some fun. Do something different. A bunch of us will be down there. Everyone would love to see you."

Torrance couldn't help but grin. Malloy, the great facilitator. The guy knew how to get along with everyone, and he knew how to fade into the distance when it was best for him. For a moment,

Torrance was jealous.

The work in front of him whispered taunts, but even he was smart enough to know it wasn't going to get done. And for all his bluster, Malloy was right. Torrance could use something to get his mind back on track, and the fact was that he needed the rounds to keep his marksmanship rating up. He was behind on his trials, and it wouldn't do to give Romanov anything else to use against him.

Surely he could spare an hour?

It wasn't like the work was going anywhere without him, and it wasn't like he had anything else to do later.

"When are you going?" he said.

"Thirty minutes?"

"Okay. I'll be there."

Abke broke the connection.

Torrance stood and stepped around his desk.

"Save my work, Abke," he said as he left.

He stopped back at his quarters to slip into a pair of loose-fitting exercise pants and a heavy fleece shirt open at the collar.

Fifteen minutes later he was the first to arrive at the range.

It was a small place, considering its purpose.

The ship had three weaponry centers. One for Shipboard Energy Projection Weapons (SEPW), a Martial Arts Center (MAC) for hand-to-hand physical combat, and this one, the Handheld Energy Projection Weapon (HEPW) systems—specifically handguns.

Acronyms are us.

Four stalls were built at the near end, sturdy black structures of anodized metal with waist-high walls separating the shooters. Sighting rods were built into the corners of each stall, ammunition wells lined shelves along the side of each cubby, and a cleaning station was built into the back of the room. Torrance couldn't actually see the anti-plasma insulation shielding that wrapped around the entire range compartment to protect the ship from errant blasts, but he felt its presence around him as an uncomfortable shell. He didn't like the idea of such a blanket right now. It made him feel trapped.

He hadn't shot for weeks, so he decided to use his free time by cleaning his weapon.

"I need my gun, Abke," Torrance said.

He pressed his thumb to the DNA lockpad and waited for Abke to confirm he was the proper requestor.

The service bay slid open, and his gun was proffered. It was a Carson semi, a powerful 38-watt plasma handgun the service provided to crew members who might participate in ground maneuvers.

The weapon was heavy and cold in his hand as he pulled the power bolt to check its safety lock. It was capable of multiple settings—a theoretically nonlethal stage that would block nerve impulses of a human target, a scattered energy beam that created a defensive burn radius designed to diffuse incoming energy projectiles, and a focused beam that took a measured charge of the energy that remained in the munitions cell and fired it in a tight-focused beam that some of the crew called "kill or drill."

Interstellar Command assigned each crew member a weapon, and required each to do periodic range work or lose their rating. Torrance had been excited when he was first assigned weapon detail, but that had changed after a bit. Shooting targets at the range was generally boring, and he really had no interest in shooting anything else.

He turned the gun over.

He didn't have enough time to break it down completely, so he did a simple contact cleanse and rubdown, then checked his charge levels.

"Beat us here, eh?" Ensign Whalen said as she and Olissy stepped into the room.

"Good afternoon, Hallie…Helen."

Malloy was thirty seconds behind them.

"Hey, LC."

"Karl."

The others went to get their weapons. Torrance picked a magazine from the ammo rack and slipped it into the weapon with a satisfying click.

"So," Malloy said when he came to stand next to Torrance. "What's up with you and Lieutenant Harthing? All the guys want to know."

Olissy and Whalen glanced up with translucent expressions of mixed concern and expectation.

The air in the room got staler, and the walls seemed to close in on him.

"Why?"

Malloy smiled. "Just nosy, I guess."

"I guess," Torrance said, ignoring them with a shrug as he stepped to the third stall to avoid the question.

He slid on a pair of shielded glasses, pushed protective plugs into both ears, and took his position.

Malloy, apparently deciding not to press the point, stepped into the stall between Torrance and the wall. Whalen and Olissy took the first and second stalls.

The target was square and split into multicolored regions.

Torrance aimed at the center and pressed the trigger.

The gun kicked and a soft thump came through his ear baffle. A ball of blue-green light streaked across the range, and a hole appeared in the blue zone in the far-left corner of the target.

Torrance curled his lips in disgust.

He was rusty.

Practice protocol called for a single shot, followed by analysis prior to the next shot—though the analysis period was generally used to jawbone with whoever else was shooting. But Torrance had no patience for analysis today.

Instead, he shot again.

This time the blast hit a green area to the right.

Shit.

A sense of angry purpose surged through him. It was a basic urge that scrubbed his mind and made the weapon feel good as the room filled up with the astringent scent of plasma residue.

He aimed and shot.

Aimed and shot.

Aimed and shot.

The odor grew strong enough to eat at the lining of his nostrils.

Something released inside him, and he shot again and again.

He aimed and shot.

Aimed and shot.

With each pulse the weapon made him feel better. Each hole in the target carried a powerful sense of righteousness that made his chest expand.

What the hell did he care about Marisa?

Aim, fire. Kickback.

What did he care about his job?

Aim, fire. Kickback.

His life?

Aim, fire. Kickback.

What about his promotion?

Was he just supposed to waste his life away fixing toilets and patching code while everyone else passed him by?

His hand became one with the weapon.

Aim, fire. Kickback. Aim, fire. Kickback.

Was he supposed to let a life-form die? Is that what Marisa wanted? Well, screw her, and screw Romanov.

Aim, fire. Kickback.

A hole blossomed in the red center.

Again.

Again.

Again.

The target shredded to tatters under a hail of plasma that fell like hammer blows. Metallic rapture coursed through Torrance's veins with each shot.

Then the magazine clicked empty.

His jaw was clenched tight.

Torrance breathed a deep sigh of release.

Malloy, Olissy, and Whalen stood with slack-jawed expressions.

"Sorry," he said, embarrassment growing. "Guess I got carried away."

Olissy cleared her throat.

The gun was hot in his hand. He pulled off his goggles, ripped the plugs from his ears, and stepped back to the controller to put his weapon back into its stall. Then he stomped away from the range.

Malloy was right, he thought.

He needed that.

NEWS

SOURCE: INFOWAVE -- NEWS for the twenty-third century
RECEIVED: July 24, 2207 UGIS EVERGUARD
TRANS DATE: March 13, 2206, Earth Standard
HEADLINE: Universe Three Destroys 1 UG Spacecraft, Hijacks 2

In an unprovoked attack executed on the day of "Starburst," the coordinated mission featuring launches of all four of the United Government's new Excelsior class Star Drive spacecraft, terrorist faction Universe Three (U3) destroyed UGIS Sunchaser *and hijacked UGIS* Icarus *and UGIS* Einstein. *Of the four spacecraft launched, only UGIS* Orion *returned safely to UG territory.*

Casualty reports were unavailable, but an anonymous source told Infowave that "it isn't good."

UGIS Sunchaser *was the ship that executed the first official faster-than-light mission undertaken by Interstellar Command, that mission being to retrieve Admiral Robert Hatch from the UGIS* Everguard.

Universe Three founder Casmir Francis issued a brief statement regarding the attack: "Where there is no dissent, there can be no freedom." He has previously stated that he and his supporters created his organization as a response to "the oppressive loss of freedom represented by the unmitigated power wielded by the United Government."

Speaking before an emergency session of the collected country-

states, Supreme President Laney Mubadid called U3 a terrorist organization and asked for authority to engage them as enemies at war.

The request was passed 123-2, with thirteen abstentions.

Planetary votes will be received and compiled over the next few days, but UG forces are already scrambling in anticipation of the results.

CHAPTER 25

UGIS *Everguard*
Ship Local Date: Jul 24, 2207
Ship Local Time: 0615

Radio transmissions are their own form of time machines.

Given *Everguard*'s travel speed and the speed of light, this horrendous attack had happened nearly three standard years ago, but the news was just catching up to them.

Torrance kept the news link turned up so he could hear it while he showered, standing in stunned silence while globs of water wobbled in the air for the few perceptible moments the artificial gravity system took to identify them and hook into their atomic structures well enough to pull them down.

It was like someone had just punched his gut.

This was impossible, yet not impossible at all.

The news played on.

Several hundred people, maybe a couple thousand across all three ships, almost certainly dead—friends of his, probably, though he didn't have the ships' rosters on hand.

He recalled the majestic chill of seeing *Sunchaser* off the observation deck. Interstellar Command had been at war since almost the moment she left *Everguard*'s side, and due to the effects of sub-luminal time dilation, they had never known.

He grabbed his towel and dried off.

Damage reports and news of casualties rolled in. Every piece of news drove home the fact that *Sunchaser* was gone and that *Einstein* and *Icarus* were lost to U3.

God damn it, he thought as he got dressed.

God Freaking Damn It.

Torrance sat in his office later that morning, staring without focus at the walls as news feeds played the same story over and over again.

No one was getting much work done.

The dream had been a thousand gleaming ships with a thousand glorious colonies inhabiting a thousand new worlds. The dream had been human beings in the Arcturus system working with people in the Scorpius cluster sharing ideas with those in the Rigel system.

The dream was finding another form of life.

Developing an understanding of the universe.

Giving human beings the stars.

This is what *Everguard*'s mission had been about. It was what each of the crew had dedicated so much of their lives to.

But humans are complex creatures. They are individuals of different tastes, different abilities, and different thoughts, and not all are so easily swayed. And it turns out that it takes only a few to derail the dream.

Now Torrance sat alone in his office, feeling hollow, powerless, and angry.

"Excuse me, Lieutenant Commander. May I have a word?"

Torrance gave a start as he came out of his fog.

It was Security Officer Casey.

Torrance's heart gave a jump.

Casey stood primly in the doorway, his dark uniform buttoned to the chin, his hands held primly behind his back. The security officer's hair was still short—Torrance had never seen it any other way, and for just a flash he wondered if Casey had it trimmed back a day's growth at a time.

"No," Torrance said, then realized with awkward hesitation that the use of the negative in that response was wrong. "That's fine," he said, standing partially and waving Casey to his other chair. "What I meant was 'No, I don't mind.' Come in, please."

It was only when Casey sat down that Torrance realized that two of his security officers had accompanied him. They took positions outside Torrance's office, their backs to the glassy section of the walls.

"Is everything all right?" Torrance said, feeling suddenly anxious.

"I hope so," Casey replied. His eyes were piercing.

"What do you mean?"

The security officer stared Torrance down for a moment as if deciding how to proceed, then went directly for the jugular. "I need to know if you had something to do with the attacks on the Excelsior class spacecraft."

"What?"

"I asked if you participated in the attacks on *Sunchaser*…et al."

"Is this a joke?"

"The twelfth wormhole pod had a failure. Did you use that pod to transfer information that might have made it easier for Universe Three to sabotage our spacecraft?"

"No!"

"Do you have any alliance or other association with Casmir Francis or any other member of Universe Three?"

"Seriously," Torrance said, his brain clutching at straws. "What is this? As you suggesting I'm a traitor?"

"I asked if you have had any alliance or other association with Casmir Francis or any other member of Universe Three. Have you had any association with him at any time of your life?"

The sound of random white noise of the office outside seeped into the suddenly quiet room. Status lights flashed in the background of Torrance's vision, and a canned voice message about the ventilation cleaning schedule spoke in the haze. His staff was aware that Casey was in his office, and was probably able to hear the interrogation.

"All I know about Casmir Francis is that I hope the UG has already hunted him down and ripped apart everything the man holds dear."

Casey looked at him sideways. "That's harsh for you, isn't it?"

"Is it?" Torrance said.

Casey raised his eyebrows just a bare notch.

"All right," Torrance continued. "Maybe it is harsh. But it's how I feel right now."

"So you have not had any contact with Universe Three?"

"No."

"How can I believe you?"

"I don't understand."

But Torrance *was* beginning to understand something. He had made a career out of seeing things in people that they didn't even know themselves, and right now he saw a man who was as defeated and as powerless as Torrance was feeling. The difference between them was that Casey was beholden to a certain hierarchy, and that this hierarchy had expectations of a shipboard officer that had nothing to do with their stated mission. Add that Casey was paid to have a predilection to paranoia and conspiracy theory, and it added up to say that Government Security Officer Malcolm Casey was worried about his job.

It was possible Casey was acting on orders. It was also possible he was working on his own in anticipation of those orders, or just working his way down on his own personal warpath because he realized that if he didn't do the footwork someone else would. It was also possible Casey was just angry, and that searching for enemies, saboteurs, or spies let him take out his frustrations.

Regardless, there was no doubt that Casey would eventually use any information he could find to save his own neck.

"I'm thinking," Casey said, "it might be best if you volunteered to come to security bay and subject yourself to some testing."

"You're just out hunting, aren't you?" Torrance regretted the question even as it left his lips.

Casey's forward lean was barely perceptible.

"Why do you ask it that way?"

"I'm sorry. I didn't mean anything by that."

"Yes, you did."

Torrance stammered.

"You think I am on a wild goose chase, is that right?"

The security officer waited. The fire in his eyes took Torrance's breath away.

"I don't know enough about anything to have an opinion, sir."

Casey sat back.

"This is my job, Lieutenant Commander. I am responsible for protecting the United Government, and I am responsible for protecting its assets and its people. While you are busy fixing heaters and changing the toilet tissue, I am busy finding spies and searching for truth."

"I understand, sir."

"Do you?"

"Yes, sir."

"I will expect you in security bay at 1530."

"I haven't done anything, sir."

"That means you will pass."

Torrance pressed his lips together.

"If you do not appear at your allotted slot," said Casey, "I will have you placed under arrest and held until such a time as we can find another suitable slot."

"I'll speak with the captain," Torrance said. "If he agrees, I'll be happy to arrange a session with you."

"The captain has the 1700 slot."

Casey stood, brushing a nonexistent speck of lint from the elbow of his uniform, then glancing up to watch the expression on Torrance's face.

"I understand," Torrance said as he, too, stood. "I assume that will be all."

"Yes," Security Officer Casey said. "I'll see you at 1530."

"Thank you, sir."

The security officer stepped out of the room, and his two goons followed him without a word.

Torrance stood alone in the silence.

Outside in Systems Command, news loops ran on screens that usually held rows of data from the ship's central systems. The staff glanced at him from the corner of their eyes. Torrance shut down his display and stepped onto the gunmetal platform outside his office. He leaned on the rail, watching his team work with silent professionalism.

Normally a steady echo of voices would fill the open space, or the sounds of bumps and crashes of equipment being moved would be ringing out from below, or the flickering shine of some system being tested would be coming from a lab room. But now everything was muted, as if the pit was more graveyard than system center.

Several of his team stared absently at their displays, doing their best to get on with their jobs. The cleaning station was unattended.

Three more years, Torrance thought. More than that, in reality. The mission had nearly three and a half more local years to finish its travels home.

He wondered what else had already happened back in the Solar System that hadn't yet traveled the proper distance for them to discover.

Did the UG even exist now? Did Earth exist?

Were his family alive?

Had U3 done permanent damage?

He thought about Marisa, and realized how much he missed her.

She had been right, of course. Given their different paths, there was no way they could be together now. But he liked her. He respected her dedication, and that she was true to her mission. He wanted to be like her, but of course he wasn't.

He thought about the Eden files.

Torrance had last picked through them only two hours ago. He hadn't discovered anything new, of course, but they helped him get his mind off the moment.

Would Casey's inquisition discover them?

Probably. He had been "lucky" enough once, but the game had changed. Casey's approach would be much more pointed now. If Casey found him lying about the files this time, he might as well go straight to the brig. The security officer was already trying to link the lost pod to some arcane concept of communication with the Universe Three terrorists. If he discovered the truth about the files, what would he twist their existence to mean? Nothing good, he was sure.

He didn't know what to do.

If he talked about them outright, he could probably never work on them again. But if he didn't say anything, it would be even worse if Romanov give him up an hour later.

Casey was like a bulldog that suddenly found a bone in his mouth and the scent of blood in his nostrils.

There was really only one answer.

He was going to have to stop studying the files.

He was going to have to tell Casey the truth and let the facts speak for themselves.

Beyond having the files destroyed and losing his access, he

would be chastised for wantonly destroying the twelfth wormhole pod and be ridiculed for thinking life existed on Eden. He would almost certainly be discharged, too, but better to be a ridiculed fool with a discharge than a railroaded traitor who spends his life in the brig.

He sighed.

He would have to cut Kitchell off, too, of course.

That would kill him a little, too. In the time they had been working together young Thomas had brought a whole different energy to the process. They had created a completely new filtering system together, and had even managed to make something that looked like a cohesive signal out of the mess—though none of the linguistic routines or other pattern-matching algorithms they had onboard were able to make it mean anything.

He would miss working with the boy, if you could call the young man a boy anymore.

Malloy came up the steps and stood at the rail next to Torrance. Like the rest of the crew, he was anxious.

"Some day, huh?"

"Yeah," Torrance replied.

"I can't believe it."

"Think of all those people."

"Shame."

Torrance nodded, but didn't say anything more. They stood like this for several moments, silent and gazing over the command because there was nothing else to do.

"Are you okay, LC? Can I do anything for you?"

"I'm fine," Torrance said. "Why do you ask?"

"I figure it's never good to see the government security officer in your CO's office."

Torrance nodded. Until now he thought the pallor across the team was completely due to the news, but Malloy brought up a good point. He needed to consider the affect Casey's presence would have on them. He looked at Malloy and realized Malloy had the crew's ear.

"I'm fine," Torrance said. "It's nothing, really."

Malloy raised one eyebrow. "Need to talk?"

"The GSO is just doing his job."

"Will we all get visits?"

Torrance smirked. "I don't know, Karl. I suspect Casey will stay at the command level to start with. But he's UG all the way through, you know? If he thinks he's got a mole somewhere, I suppose he'll start digging."

"Yeah, I know."

"Tell the folks it'll be okay, though, all right? Tell them I said to just do the right thing and keep their minds on the work. We've still got a long ways to go. Everything will work out."

"All right," Malloy said, staring out over the team. "I'll let them know."

"Thanks."

They stood for another moment.

"Guess I should head on to Forward," Malloy finally said.

Torrance nodded. He was doing a lot of nodding today, it seemed. It helped him avoid talking.

Malloy left and Torrance immediately felt better.

He wrapped his hands around the rail. The clock on the wall displayed shift time.

Three and a half years, he thought.

That was a suddenly a very long time.

He turned and went back to his office.

"Abke," he said, "please ask Thomas Kitchell to come here."

Chapter 26

UGIS *Everguard*
Ship Local Date: September 30, 2207
Ship Local Time: 1945

"You called, sir?"

It was Thomas Kitchell. He was tall and still borderline thin, still growing into his body despite crossing out of his teens. He would be eligible to formally enter the service when they arrived home, and Torrance knew he had plans to do so. *"I want to run big shipboard systems,"* he told Torrance a month ago. *"And it seems like that's the best path."*

Torrance hadn't argued with him.

"Yes," he replied. "Come in. We've got something to talk about."

Kitchell entered and came to stand beside Torrance at his desk. There was a practiced ease in the way he looked over Torrance's shoulder to stare at the code.

The hooded projection display carried a fractal image that shifted in a strange loopy wave that seemed to almost have a rhythm.

"What is this?" Kitchell asked.

"Abke," Torrance said. "Please shut the door."

"What's wrong?" Kitchell said as the door shut.

"This is your own master systems security key."

The boy looked at him with the obvious question clearly etched on his expression. "Why are you showing me this?"

"I had a meeting with Officer Casey this morning."

"So?"

"He's looking for things he can find to connect our mission to the U3 attack. I'm afraid of what he'll do if he finds I'm hiding files from him, so I'm going to tell him about what I've been doing."

"But…he'll stop you."

"Yes, he will."

"We're so close. We can't stop now."

"No," Torrance said, looking to the display and the shimmering security key. "We can't."

Kitchell gave Torrance a quizzical glance. "I don't understand."

"I have to stop working with these files. But that doesn't mean someone else can't keep going."

"You can't mean …" Kitchell glanced back at the key.

"You've earned my trust, Thomas. I've put this key in your private memory space. I want you to find a quiet place. There's not much time, so it has to happen now. Copy everything into a separate storage. Don't tell me where. I don't want to give it away. When you're done, save it using this key."

Kitchell was silent. His gaze flickered to the screen, then back to Torrance.

"They're going to strip your space."

"Right."

"What happens if the GSO comes after me?"

"If you do what I say, I think my confession, combined with Romanov's word, will give Casey a complete story. No one else knows you're involved. Casey will probably take the files for evidence before he has someone kill my space. If he's got the files and his people tell him they cleaned my space, I think that will be enough to shut the door on any further investigation."

"And if not?"

Torrance shrugged. "Just do it."

Kitchell nodded.

"Can we still do the work together?"

"Maybe," Torrance replied. The mere fact that Kitchell asked made him feel good. "In a while, anyway. Maybe after the heat dies down. Or maybe not. Maybe it'll have to be you working alone. I don't know."

"Take a chance, right?"

"Say that when you're the one talking to Casey."

Kitchell pulled his lips into a frown.

"Right now I think we focus on saving the data in a place you can access it."

"All right," Kitchell said.

"You know how to use the key?"

"Yeah," the boy replied with a grin that made him look twelve. "I know how to use it."

CHAPTER 27

UGIS *Everguard*
Ship Local Date: September 30, 2207
Ship Local Time: 1530

Government Security Officer Casey's office was cold, as always. But that wasn't why Torrance shivered as he sat down.

The chair was comfortable, but arranged to face into a rounded "corner" of the room. The electromagnetic scanners had already been placed on stands and focused on the area where his head would be. Sensor pads were already affixed to areas his hands would rest.

The scanners would let the interrogators watch Torrance's brainwaves fire as he responded to the security officer's questions. The sensor pads would provide fine resolution to the vital sign data that was already coming from the e-lint systems.

"You don't really have to go to this extent, sir," Torrance said. "I'll tell you the truth regardless."

Casey smiled, but directed the secondary officer to sit.

By regulations, no full scan could happen without a secondary officer in the area to confirm proper procedure—as if the secondary officer would actually say anything if Casey went out of bounds.

It didn't matter, though.

Torrance had decided to tell the truth, so that's what he did.

* * *

For sixty minutes Torrance responded to questions, and for sixty minutes he dug his own grave. When the examination was complete, he didn't need Malcolm Casey to tell him that his career was officially over.

He would serve out the mission, then he would be discharged without comment—which is not really different from being discharged dishonorably, except employers needed to create a different reason to not hire you.

"Thank you for your time," the Security Officer said when he was finished with the examination. "You can return to your post."

Arrival

Chapter 28

UGIS *Everguard*
Ship Local Date: September 14, 2211
Ship Local Time: 1015

Aldrin Station
Local Date: December 21, 2214
Station Local Time: 1941

A lot changes in fifteen years.

Everguard had finished its deceleration, entered the Solar System, and looped its way over the asteroid belt. As the craft taxied closer to Luna's Aldrin Station, Torrance found more of his time taken up monitoring the shield that protected the ship's ancient hull from the millions of bits of space debris that littered the area.

Tomorrow afternoon *Everguard* would dock, and the crew would formally cross the three-and-a-quarter-year relativistic date line it would take to rejoin society. Eighteen Sol standard years would have passed in Luna Local rather than the fifteen they had experienced in local time. There were people to see again, places to visit, and politics to catch up on. War was raging, if such can be said about interstellar warfare with a small guerilla-style enemy.

But first there was a party to attend.

* * *

Romanov delivered the after-dinner keynote address, wherein he said all the right things and thanked all the right people. The lights dimmed and a documentary of their mission played, complete with the trumped-up drama of the launch failure. Then the festivities began.

The music blared so loudly that dancers had to yell into each other's ears.

Being that it was Earth standard Christmastime, Santa hats were suddenly the fashion of choice, and couples made liberal use of mistletoe that hung from the rafters. The aroma of liquor and human exertion heated the darkened hall to the point where Torrance found it hard to breathe.

A blue banner with crisp white letters proclaiming "Happy Mega-Leap Day" was draped behind the podium.

"Can you effin' believe it?" Malloy said, tipping a gin and tonic and slurring his words as he pointed at the data screen built into the bar counter.

A schedule of junkets out of Aldrin Station filled its display:

DEC 22 - 0930: JUMPSHIP TO EUROPA
DEC 22 - 1545: SHUTTLE TO MARS COLONY DELIAN
DEC 23 - 1215: EXPEDITION TO MIRANDA
DEC 24 - 0715: SCIENTIFIC SKIFF TO THE PLUTO-CHARON BINARY

"We made it, eh?" Torrance replied.

"Hard to believe, ain't it?"

He nodded and sipped his bourbon and water—the idea that one-day jaunts across the Solar System had become routine enough to put on a transit schedule was mind-boggling. He had selected the drink because it was something quick and direct that wouldn't pussyfoot around when it came to getting him drunk. Torrance didn't really want to be here, but the captain had ordered all hands to attend and Malloy had convinced him it was his duty to tip a few for old times' sake.

So, like, what the hell, eh?

Like everyone else, it was his last night on the ship.

Unlike most, Torrance knew it was his last night in the service.

Romanov had been chastised, and would pay for his part in the wormhole pod deception by taking a crappy assignment on a shuttle. But Torrance was gone. He assumed that his status as the guy who pushed the button to launch the pods was the one thing that kept his discharge as better than dishonorable.

The music filled space around them, the bass pounded against his brain. Dance music.

Malloy tipped his drink and pointed at tomorrow's guest list.

"You see that shit?" he said. "Ambassador. Ambassador. Ambassador. *Another* goddamned ambassador. *Assistant* to the goddamned ambassador. Ambassador's delegate. We created this world. You would think we ought to rate at least a goddamned vice president, for crying out loud."

Torrance snickered. "Don't knock it. Luna's grand marshal will be here."

"Yeah, right." Malloy swirled his drink and slammed back the last of it. "The grand marshal. Now there's a real quark on the butt of society. I'll bet every one of the poor bastards who got roped into this weren't even aware we were coming until a week ago."

"Why do you say that?"

He gritted his teeth. "Just a hunch."

Torrance nodded. "I hear ya, Karl. The world's had FTL for long enough now that no one cares about us anymore, except maybe as museum pieces."

"Well, they damned well *should*. They'll regret ignoring us. Someday they will. Maybe earlier than you think."

"What do you mean?"

Malloy shrugged and gave a drunken smile.

"What an effin' crock this Star Drive stuff is, anyway, eh? We give 'em the effin' galaxy and all they do is make a new batch of politicians to go scrambling for more effin' real estate. If we had to do it over again, I think it would be better to send those goddamned pods right back up Hatch's ass."

Torrance laughed and took a drink.

"Christ, Karl. Look at us."

"So, what are you going to do?" Malloy said, picking an ice cube out of his glass to suck on.

It was a question he'd heard at least a hundred times the past month. *What are you going to do?* More than two thousand crew members and families were buzzing about what came next. It made the entire last stint of the mission feel like senior year, spring semester.

Torrance gave Malloy a sideways glance, and thought about the Eden files.

Casey surprised him earlier today with the news that the original files hadn't been destroyed, that instead the security officer had ordered them stored away in a place Torrance couldn't get to until they docked. Sadistic little bastard. He wasn't sure exactly why Casey did that, except that it had soon become obvious the data itself wasn't dangerous in any way—only the fact that he had used it to justify sabotaging a mission and destroying government property mattered. The magnanimous expression on the security officer's face earlier this morning made it clear that Casey thought he was being quite generous, so Torrance figured the gift was just a way for Casey to feel better about being his sorry-assed self.

Casey had never discovered that Kitchell had his own copy of the data and that Kitchell had been digging through it in fits and starts throughout the last legs of the trip. He didn't know that Kitchell had beaten him to the punch and created a copy of the files encoded on a data crystal that Torrance held in his pocket even as Casey was providing his self-congratulatory form of charity.

Not that it really mattered.

Even with Kitchell's quick mind and miraculous methods of finding advanced routines, they needed better tools and more time. Without full access to the Signal Processing Lab and with only a few hours here and there to work with, there was only so much they could do.

The kid was brilliant, though.

He was going to do something special, that was for certain.

Kitchell was twenty-two years old, now. He had been just past seven when the mission launched. After serving his volunteer stint, he had officially joined the command as an auxiliary member a year and a half ago, and done a remarkable job. Like everyone his age or younger, *Everguard* was probably the only home he really remembered.

It was going to be fun to see what happened to the kid. He wanted to see what kind of chances Kitchell would take, and where those chances would carry him. Torrance hoped they would have a long relationship.

He didn't know much about what his own future held, but he knew it would still have something to do with a search for life on Eden. Free from the restrictions of the military, and with a little money stored away, maybe he would finally be able to spend long, concerted hours digging everywhere.

In the end, he couldn't help himself. No matter that his studies were turning up empty, he felt a presence on the planet. As crazy as other people might say he was, he believed.

So, yeah, he would work with the Eden files.

But he wasn't going to tell Malloy that.

"I don't know what I'm going to do," he replied. "What about you?"

Malloy swirled the last of the ice in his glass, motioned to the bartender, and tossed off a shrug. "Probably hit France and Italy for a couple weeks first."

"Really?"

"My dad always told stories about France and Italy. Figure they'll probably be as good a place to hang around as any. For a while, anyway. Besides," he said, his smile gleaming, "after a decade and a half cooped up on this ship I think I need to look at a few different women."

"Well, I hear they've got 'em different there."

Malloy's grin widened, and the bartender set a fresh drink in front of him. "Maybe after that I'll get into the Eta Cass thing."

He was talking about the war.

Universe Three had established a base in the Eta Cassiopeia system, and the news was full of sporadic clashes there as the United Government was still trying to save face by retrieving their stolen spacecraft.

"I don't know, Karl. That stuff sounds ugly. I mean, they're talking like it's all skimmer actions and retaliatory strikes, but the facts look like we're in a weird full-scale war that's made even weirder because it's spread out over light years."

"Yeah, I know. But it's important, don'cha think?"

Torrance nodded and took a hit from his drink.

Across the way, Marisa danced with Paul Terrano.

Those two had been an item for a while, but as *Everguard* drew closer to home Torrance could see it wouldn't last. Marisa was going to be assigned to a new Star Drive system. Paul was an Ag specialist who worked in *Everguard*'s Horticultural Command—a service that FTL travel had rendered essentially obsolete.

Torrance sighed.

At least he had patched things up between them enough that she talked to him. She was smart, and interesting. He had enjoyed her friendship over the past three years. Turns out she gave pretty good advice.

"She'll leave him, too," Malloy said.

"What?"

"I said—"

Torrance waved him off. "I know," he said. "It's all right. Really, it is."

"Hey, screw 'em, right?" Malloy said, holding his glass up for a toast Torrance was supposed to join in.

Torrance tipped his glass, drank the diluted dregs of bourbon, and put it down. "I'm turning in."

"So early?"

"Yeah."

Malloy stood and held his hand out.

"I'm sure I'll see you tomorrow, LC. But just in case."

Torrance nodded and took Malloy's hand. He didn't have any great words to share, and that made him feel even more embarrassed.

"Be good, Karl."

"Aye, sir."

That night or, technically, early the next morning, he slipped into his bed on *Everguard* for the last time.

As directed, he had packed his wardrobe and all his essentials before the party. They fit in three boxes that were now stacked in a makeshift tower just inside his doorway. The ship stewards would take them in the morning.

The sheets were cool, but heavy on his skin.

Darkness was nearly total.

"Play audio file K-12, Abke."

The sound came low, a gentle hiss that reminded him of waves on the beach. It was an audio rendition of the Eden "storm" he had made in the old days. It was the one file Kitchell had retooled and repackaged, then slipped to Torrance a long time ago. The white noise was like Mozart or Bach as far as he was concerned. Though it didn't contain any clear pattern, his brain felt rhythms and melodies in the white fuzz. In the edgy darkness of his quarters, Torrance Black thought about the pod he had left behind, the single piece of equipment he had diverted to the planet known as Eden.

It had been a long time ago.

How long would it take an intelligent species to re-engineer a system like that? What kind of physics would they need to know? For a moment he thought about Adrienne—remarried with three kids now. He thought about Marisa. He thought about life in general.

Everguard's mission was complete.

His career was finished.

What *would* he do now?

The question lingered until he fell asleep.

Chapter 29

UGIS *Everguard*
Ship Local Date: September 15, 2211
Ship Local Time: 1015

Torrance had to be on the bridge for the docking ceremony in fifteen minutes, but right now he was in his office, watching the team work for the very last time. They were in their traditional whites today. He used to love the precision of that look, but now it made him feel like a starched mannequin.

Many display screens displayed Aldrin Station as it hung outside the observation port, looking like a silver spider against the black sky. It orbited Luna at Lagrange point 4, its spindlelike access corridors turning silent cartwheels in space, its docking pods glistening like dew with the sunlight.

System parameters flowed over the data screen embedded in his office wall. Everything looked good—power distribution, ionic filtration, environmental controls—all exactly where they were supposed to be. The computer systems were up. Docking mechanicals were on standby. Even the damned toilets were in perfect shape.

Trimming rockets fired as they drew nearer.

He locked the ship's external service bots into their maintenance bays via the remote interface.

It was a sad chore, actually. Putting his toys away, knowing they would almost certainly never be used again. He sighed and picked a plaque off the wall. *UGIS Everguard - Changing the Universe*, the inscription read. He flipped it over and scanned the names of his teammates.

The comm panel beeped.

Captain Romanov's voice echoed through the compartment.

"Ladies and gentlemen, crewmates of the finest rank. Estimated time to completion of this mission is forty-five Earth standard minutes. Please do me the great honor of taking your docking positions. It has been an honor to cruise with you."

Torrance opened his personal duffel and slipped the plaque into the bag. Straightening, he ran his hands down the hips of his pants, feeling the hard edge of the data crystal there. He pulled his hat from its compartment, and stepped onto the gunmetal platform outside.

He took one last look around the command, breathed one more breath of its air, and walked through the doorway that led to the central corridor—which was a twisting path that led through various commands and offices, and toward the lift tube that would take him to the bridge. It was a long walk, but this time he enjoyed every moment of it, trying to soak in the moment. He passed the storage bays and the deck's physical fitness center. As he passed the shooting range, the memory of his very bad day came to him. It seemed a long time ago. Ahead of him, corridors that connected the deck to living quarters merged from the right, Pod Engineering was ahead to the left.

As he strolled, the flickering of the lights were the first sign that something was wrong.

Torrance paused, frowning.

What could have caused that?

Then the emergency horns began to blare.

Chapter 30

UGIS *Everguard*
Ship Local Date: September 15, 2211
Ship Local Time: 1017

The tooth-grinding groan of ripping metal screeched through the hallway. An alarm shrieked like a banshee's wail. The floor warped and rolled like it was made of rubber beneath his feet.

Suddenly Torrance was flying through the air.

The lights went out.

He was on the floor, his arm numb and tingling beneath him, his ears ringing.

Then the pressure of the artificial gravity system was gone, and he felt like he was floating.

Voices came from everywhere, some screaming and crying, some yelling orders. The emergency lights cast scarlet-brown shadows across the darkness. Cold pain shot up his arm when he tried to move.

A broken wrist, maybe?

His head swam in throbbing pain.

He put his good hand to his temple and found his hat was gone and his forehead was tender.

An acidic odor filled the corridor. Electrical fire, Torrance thought.

The lights flickered again, and he realized he was floating in microgravity. Yes. He was. The grav system was dead.

A woman struggled to move up the hallway, her fluorescent white uniform stained crimson by the emergency lighting. Her arms and legs kicked in a windmilling motion that made it look like she might be swimming. A long strand of her dark hair had worked its way loose to coil around her like a snake hanging from a tree.

The emergency siren grew beyond annoying.

"You okay, LC?" Lieutenant Malloy was at his side, holding Torrance by the shoulder. His eyes were uncharacteristically wide.

"What happened, Karl?"

"Something blew. We got no power over three-quarters of the ship. The monitor array is blank. We need to check Forward." He used the ceiling handrail for leverage and lugged Torrance toward the command deck.

Torrance grabbed hold of the rail with his good hand. "No," he said.

"Come on, LC."

"Not that way," Torrance said.

He pulled himself from Malloy's grip and turned back to Systems Command. He needed to know what was going on. Something was catastrophically wrong, and he had to see data from the entire ship to figure out what it was.

Malloy argued, but his words faded into the alarm's drone.

Smoke filled the corridor with the thick smell of burned electronics.

Torrance swung toward a bulkhead thirty meters away, pulling his throbbing hand close to his chest.

What had happened to cause something like this?

A collision?

That didn't make sense. Except for Aldrin Station and the moon itself, there was nothing out there that could hit *Everguard* hard enough to cause this kind of damage.

Even a major hull breach from something smaller should be easily contained.

Forward Deck, where Malloy wanted to head, contained the admiral's bridge and was designed as a series of vacuum-tight compartments in case they hit something too large for the magnetic shield to handle. Every passage to and from there was outfitted with automatic seals that would shut down to compartmentalize any loss of vacuum, and routine diagnostics ran daily to ensure everything was active and functional.

Central Deck, the thick, bulbous portion of the craft where all vital life-sustaining systems were maintained and where most of the day-to-day work was done, had been built to similar standards but with larger sections. A breach there would damage more area, but was no more likely to cascade into a global problem than one in Forward Deck. The rearward compartments housed the crew and their families. The weakest points in the structure were the collection of six equally spaced, enriched-titanium struts that affixed the ship's collider drive to Central Deck—but they should be under almost no stress at this point in the flight.

So, what the hell was going on?

It had to be something big.

They stepped into Systems Command, Torrance first, Malloy right behind.

The area was functioning on emergency power, and the backup artificial gravity system acquired them as they crossed into the room. Several consoles were still in the process of reinitializing.

The frantic crew examined screens and spoke in terse voices.

"Status," Torrance said, his voice firm, but drowned in the din as he climbed the stairs that led to the main floor.

The siren blared another two bleats as Torrance scanned the room.

The ache in his wrist surged.

"I said I need status," he said again, this time loud enough to carry over the bleating siren.

Heads swung around and the chatter came to a halt.

He turned to find Thomas Kitchell standing at the command station—wide-eyed and excited, but obviously in control of himself. His face was drawn, his lips thin against his teeth. His blue-green eyes were vaporous in the stark emergency lighting. Young as he was, the kid was still focused.

"Systems are just coming back online, sir," Kitchell said, yelling over the sirens. "Give them a minute."

The activity seemed to settle the rest of the crew down.

Torrance felt a sensation of pride in the kid's bearing.

"All right," Torrance said. "Comm?"

Kitchell's fingers scurried over the panel. "Spotty, LC. We have links to maybe a third of the personal quarters, but they're dropping in and out. I can get contact with propulsion, too. It's all flakey, though." He shook his head absently. "I mean, it's all just flakey as hell."

"Bridge?"

"Nothing."

"Aldrin Station?"

Kitchell shook his head harder and focused on Torrance. "Nothing there, either, sir—I'm working on it, though."

Torrance peered at the screen.

"Show me the vacuum board," Torrance said, turning to the station that would usually be Olissy's but finding instead that Marisa Harthing was standing there.

Their gazes locked.

"Nav is dead," she explained. "Thought I could help."

There was no time to ask about Olissy.

"Good," he finally said. "Do you know how to get me the vacuum map?"

Marisa frowned. "That's not really my thing."

Torrance stepped up to the control board. The system flashed its readiness. He toggled a button, then gave his fingerprint to the security scanner.

A holo of the ship floated over the projection system.

Light-blue sections were compartments where atmosphere was detectable; black sections had sensors that were not responsive— places where vacuum had likely breached.

A gasp circled the room.

"My God," somebody whispered.

Black scars split the ship from both forward and rearward sections. Systems Command was in the middle of Central Deck, which had seen some breaching but remained intact on the whole.

Torrance's skin bristled.

The room came to a standstill under the constant pounding of the sirens, each of the crew staring with slack jaws at the image of the ship.

If this was a realistic picture, it meant more than a thousand people—anyone on the bridge, several hundred people in personal quarters, and probably a lot more—were likely dead.

The depth of the crew's silence was a lead weight on his chest.

He had led Systems Command, of course. But this was different. These people weren't looking to him for a routine command, or a direction out of the standard playbook. This team wanted him to give them something they didn't have.

Bold, he thought, as he breathed through the moment.

Bold, he thought, as he felt something click in his mind and he seemed to almost separate from his own body.

"Nothing means anything, yet," Torrance said in his firmest voice. "Something's obviously rocked the ship good and hard. It could be that the sensor system is just broken."

His words worked for a moment.

The fear permeating the room receded. But the smell of fire grew stronger, and the hologram's blackness cast a pall across the room. These were intelligent people. No one believed the blackness was a collection of bad sensors.

"Abke, I want diagnostics. And give me whatever the fire systems are reporting."

Abke didn't respond.

Torrance used his good hand to type a physical system command.

He wanted to pull up some good news. He wanted things to be back where they were just five minutes ago. But mostly, he realized, he just wanted to be seen *doing* something…anything…just as long as he wasn't fumbling around senselessly in front of the men and women he had led for so long. They had to figure out how bad this really was, and then they had to fix it.

The system spit some code, but it wasn't enough to see anything.

"I want fire reports," he said to Ensign Whalen.

"I don't have Comm in those areas," the ensign responded.

Torrance nodded. Without reliable communications, there was only one way he was going to get real information.

He turned to Marisa.

Her gaze held no fear.

"I need you to take a detail to Rearward," he said. "Karl, you take one to Forward. I need hands-on information. If these are true breaches, I expect your teams to confirm integrity of the seals and begin rescue operations. With luck, though, you'll be able to say our sensor system is just broken."

"Yes, sir," Malloy said.

Marisa nodded.

"EVA suits for both details," Torrance said. "No complaints. The grav system is down and we could be breached, so mag boots active, and no one goes into a compartment adjacent to a black zone without a suit on."

"Aye, sir," Marisa said.

Malloy moved to the EVA lockers with determination painted on his face. He, too, seemed relieved to be doing something besides standing around.

Malloy and Marisa gathered teams and assigned positions.

Engineers kept working to collect what information from their stations they could.

A few damage reports trickled in.

The power was down over most of the ship. Ten of twelve oxygen filters were dead and the other two were at limited capacity.

Torrance took a deep breath and climbed the stairs to the central control station two at a time. The station was a ten-meter square with glass panels in the upper section of the walls on all sides. He slipped behind the desk, and his wrist throbbed in the relative quiet. Red light flashed crimson on the glass panels.

He felt suddenly very alone and very violated.

He thought about the situation again.

Given the design of the vacuum containment system and the massive black blocks that filled the holographic display, if something had hit them, it had to have been something huge. But Aldrin was the only other thing out there and the relative speeds of *Everguard* and the station weren't anywhere near those required to do as much damage as the ship appeared to have suffered.

He was relieved to see Abke was responding at his personal station.

He keyed the voice system on his computer.

"Give me any vacuum diagnostic reports you can get and show me all parameters on the auto vacuum-lock routines," he said.

Information about how the system was calibrated rolled over the projector. It was weird, though. Probably only an isolated instance, he thought at first. A partial code-block. Limited depth of functionality.

More data scrolled before him, though.

Pages and pages.

It didn't take long for the pattern to say something was wrong.

Torrance spotted the anomaly, sat back, and rubbed his eyes.

When he withdrew his hand, it was shaking.

Chapter 31

UGIS *Everguard*
Ship Local Date: September 15, 2211
Ship Local Time: 1036

"Lieutenant Commander?"

Torrance looked up.

Kitchell stood in the doorway, rubbing his chin with nervous energy.

The blue and black holo of the damaged spacecraft hung in the distance behind him.

"I've got a message on port 6 I think you'll want to hear."

"Who's it from?" Torrance replied.

"It's from somewhere in Aldrin Station, sir. But it's on a common carrier, probably a system-wide broadcast. It's Universe Three."

"Universe Three?" He looked at Kitchell, shaking his head. It was too much to take in all at once.

The kid nodded. "We've been attacked, sir." Kitchell touched the comm pad.

"… the freedom of all human beings."

The voice was female and terse.

"Universe Three looks at the world as three spheres. The first is the sphere of our Solar System. The next is the sphere of our galaxy. And finally comes the sphere of all galaxies that comprise

our universe. We are dedicated to seeing human beings free to roam them all. We are dedicated to keeping the universe from being destroyed by conglomerate greed. We are dedicated to keeping governments from restricting the use of Star Drives to only those with power.

"Universe Three will lead humankind to true freedom.

"We will fight repression in every system and unjust control on every planet.

"Everguard's burned-out husk stands testament to this goal. The craft that brought us the Star Drive has been burned to cinders, just as the galactic government will be if it continues its unjust attacks on the human spirit."

Torrance sat back in his chair.

Yes, he thought. Everything made sense now. Except, of course, that nothing like this could ever make sense.

Kitchell shuffled his feet.

"Have you heard from Aldrin?" Torrance asked.

"Radio's no good at standard freqs, but we're scanning and I assume they are, too. Shouldn't be long until we link up."

"Tight-band laser?"

"Haven't tried."

"Then get on it. I want to know what they're doing right now. Tell them we have survivors and need a transport as soon as possible. When that's done, I want you to check on the availability of the escape shuttles. If nothing else, maybe we can ferry people out of here."

"Aye, sir."

Kitchell went to his comm station.

Software code and system cals glowed orange against the glass of the desktop.

The air was clammy. Voices and alarms blurred into a single buzzing whine behind him.

He gazed at the parameters again. Just to be sure.

The vacuum diagnostic wasn't there.

That meant the primary configuration file had been altered, which meant someone did this on purpose, which made sense now. The vacuum seals had been disabled. Normally a diagnostic routine would run every five minutes and send a warning directly to the service panel if such a problem were discovered.

Torrance pulled the primary job schedule.

The vacuum diagnostic wasn't there, either.

He glanced at the holo through the glass wall, then clenched his eyes tight. This was an inside job. Someone had removed the routine from the schedule, meaning it wouldn't run when it was supposed to and therefore wouldn't note the fact that the seals had been tampered with.

Bloody hell.

Both the containment system and the diagnostic program had been corrupted.

A chill shivered up his spine and his gut felt like he had eaten a brick.

Who?

How many people knew how to disable the vacuum containment system?

Kitchell.

He had given Kitchell his own goddamned key, hadn't he? Thomas Kitchell could change anything he wanted. The idea hit him like a right cross to the soul.

He raced out of his office and gripped the rail over the gunmetal platform, recoiling in pain as he accidentally tried to use his damaged hand.

The crew's faces turned his way, including Kitchell.

Torrance drew a breath to scream, but the expression on the kid's face stopped him.

No. That was impossible. After all this time it was impossible for him to believe Thomas Kitchell had done this.

But if not Kitchell, who?

Marisa? Why had she shown up? Could she have stolen his private key sometime earlier? Someone else on the staff? Oblivious to stares from his team, he glanced to the EVA closet and saw it was empty. Or maybe it could have been from outside. An image of the round-faced grin of Silvio Nivead came to him. Someone like Silvio could have done this—and someone like Silvio, whose career had been in the dustbin for decades, might well be a target for recruitment by a group like Universe Three.

Torrance cursed.

The darkening display of *Everguard*'s systems said he had a bigger issue to deal with now.

Forward Deck was gone, and Rearward nearly so.

Maybe half of Central Deck remained operational.

The pattern said that whoever did this had set explosives along the ship's external skin. With the containment system down, the decks had blown like dominoes.

But something must have gone wrong.

If the explosion had continued through the rest of Central Deck, there wouldn't have been anything at all left of *Everguard*. And that's what U3's message suggested was the plan.

They hadn't meant to leave anything behind.

Some of the bombs must not have detonated.

The crew looked at him with confused expressions. He clamored down the stairs, taking two and three at a time, cradling his sore wrist that was already stiffening to a constant ache. A film of sweat covered his brow.

The holo of the ship hung in the background, and the black void where the bridge should be seemed to give a cold chuckle.

"Are you okay, sir?" Kitchell asked.

"Have you been able to contact Aldrin?"

"Yes, sir. They're dispatching a transport as requested. But all docking locks have been damaged—essentially welded shut or blown away. They won't be able to execute rescue activity until a containment crew cuts their way in."

"Escape shuttles?" Torrance asked.

"I, uh …" Kitchell glanced at the model. "I don't think anything's left there, sir."

Air locks welded shut, shuttle bays destroyed, air handling systems struggling to meet the demand of what was certainly a leaking spacecraft—if he was right, the rest of the bombs could go off at any time, and if that happened everyone aboard *Everguard* might well be dead long before an access bay could be created.

He gave an appreciative whistle. "This guy knew what he was doing, didn't he?"

No one responded.

He wondered about Malloy and Marisa. Should he try to alert them? No. Assuming they weren't involved, alerting them would do nothing but add to their teams' sense of panic. Best to just let them go and see what they could do. He didn't want to contemplate what alerting either of them would do if they were actually involved in the attack.

"I need volunteers," he said. "I'll explain as we go, but you'll need to know we're heading toward vacuum, and, as you can see, we are fresh out of EVA suits. Ten seconds to decide. I'll take the first two who step forward."

Time stopped.

A boot hit the gunmetal floor.

Kitchell, of course. Kitchell would do anything for him. Then Yarrow.

"Okay. The rest of you operate your stations. Comms, track my path and report status to Aldrin on tight beam every five seconds."

He stepped toward the door, Kitchell and Yarrow following closely behind.

CHAPTER 32

Emergency lights flickered in the corridor.

The artificial gravity system was still dead outside Systems Command, but Torrance surmised the explosions had set what was left of *Everguard* spinning because she was rotating enough to create a false gravity along the rightmost wall. Using both the ceiling rails and the limited force of the ship's spin, Torrance, Kitchell, and Yarrow followed the corridor toward the section that remained intact.

Torrance beamed a flashlight ahead of him as best he could with his bad hand, launching himself ahead with his good one. The beam caught the smoky haze that was beginning to build in the corridor.

If he listened just right, he could still hear *Everguard* talking: the repeated clicks of relays oscillating through ventilation ducts as the air system tried to come on again, the snap of the power grid, the groans of flayed metal still folding under the power of vacuum. A metallic groan like the sound of a lonely humpback whale echoed from deep within the ship.

He knew this ship.

The thought of her savaged like this, hurtling so powerlessly through space, gave him the most singular sense of loss.

The haze blurred his vision as they got farther from Systems Command.

Three dark forms bobbed listlessly in the corridor ahead. All three were members of Malloy's team. Two were obviously dead, shot at close range, but the third clutched at the gaping wound at his throat that gurgled with each breath. Torrance didn't see Malloy anywhere.

Malloy. It was Malloy.

The certainty of it curled inside his stomach.

Malloy had access to most of the ship's support systems. He also knew enough about the craft to understand its weak points and to set charges appropriately. And Malloy was resourceful enough to understand the code behind the vacuum system. He could disable it.

Torrance saw the truth in all its glory, and that truth made him want to punch a hole in the wall.

Torrance grabbed Yarrow by the shoulder. "Do what you can for him."

The ensign nodded and went to the man.

The passage split, looping around on itself.

He turned to Kitchell.

"You take the left, I'll take the right."

Kitchell nodded.

Torrance slipped through the shaft alone. It was strange to see the place like this, empty and draped in sepia darkness.

The distant grinding from the environmental motors filled the background as they struggled to push air.

A harsh flash of white light flared ahead. It was a handheld, Torrance thought.

He cut his beam to avoid being noticed.

The place smelled of dust and warm oil.

A wall panel floated freely in the corridor before him, turning silently in the dim light like slow-motion shrapnel. It made him think of a sea ray he had seen in an aquarium once.

The flash came again.

The low glow of a light wedged into debris to provide working light was obvious now.

Malloy knelt over a package of explosives that trailed wires back into the exposed ductwork. The lieutenant's hood and helmet hung off his EVA suit and down his back. A plasma gun lay hidden in shadows near the floor beside him—Torrance assumed it was Malloy's Carson, taken illegally from the range. As if that mattered.

Malloy glanced over his shoulder.

"I figured I would see you here pretty soon, LC. Only a matter of time before you saw vacuum containment had been crashed."

The lieutenant clipped a cord in place, then pushed the explosive package back into the ductwork.

"Can you effin' believe it? The damned thing was supposed to trigger at once, but somehow this section got on a different timer run."

He removed a control box from his belt and waved it around with a false smile.

"Don't worry, though. Nothing can go wrong this time."

"Why?" Torrance said, the scope of his question obvious.

"Get your head out of your ass, LC. Nobody's getting nothing from this mission but a couple a big-assed companies and their government cronies. Meantime, the little guys like you and me, we just get shit on."

"I don't see it that way."

"No offense, LC, but you're too busy inside your own head to see anything. No one cares about nothing but their own wallets."

"There's got to be a better way."

Malloy snickered. "You're worse off than I thought."

Torrance glanced at the box.

It was a repugnant package of taped-up electronics, silver wire, and plastic explosives with a fuse that snaked along the wall and trailed into the ventilation shaft.

He flexed his hand subconsciously, letting the pain ground him and considered launching himself at Malloy.

The lieutenant pointed the Carson his way.

Something moved in the distance behind Malloy.

The yellow-white outline of Kitchell's cheek was etched in the bleeding light at the edge of Malloy's flash. The corridor curved slightly, allowing him to press against the inner wall and remain unseen by Malloy.

If Torrance could keep the lieutenant's attention, maybe

Kitchell would be able to surprise him and take the gun. Kitchell nodded as if confirming his understanding of the situation.

"It was you, wasn't it?" Torrance said, grasping at straws for ways to delay Malloy's progress.

"What?"

"The EMI while we were at Alpha Cen—the interference that stopped the first launch. You didn't want us to be successful, so you tried to stop the mission. It was you."

Malloy smirked and started to use his free hand to put his tools back into his utility belt, then thought better and just tossed them into the detritus around him. "You're still worried about that? I thought it was just a joke."

"Of course I'm worried about it, Karl. I thought it was a new species."

Malloy's laughter actually hurt more than Torrance thought it would.

"Doesn't matter now, does it?" Malloy said.

"Does to me."

Malloy stood up, Carson still trained on Torrance. He shook his head sorrowfully. "Well, in that case let me give you a gift, LC. Whatever it was out there that scrubbed that first launch, it wasn't me."

Kitchell edged closer.

"It wasn't?"

"No one thought we would ever make it that far, so we didn't plan anything for making it. At least nothing out here, anyway." Malloy toggled a frequency on the control box. "Of course, we had other things going on in case of a successful launch."

Kitchell was almost in place.

"We?"

Malloy grinned. "We look at the world as three spheres, LC."

"You're U3." Torrance kicked himself for not making the connection right away, but he had known Malloy for so long that it was hard to see him otherwise.

Malloy's only response was the gentle raising of one eyebrow.

"You'll kill yourself for *them*?" Torrance asked, trying to keep from sounding too desperate.

Malloy reached for his flashlight.

"You know me better than that, LC. I'm not some whacked-out

fanatic. I got no intention of dying today. Like I said last night—I'll be heading toward Eta Cass before too long. Just not on the side you assumed."

"That's why you weren't at Systems this morning," Torrance said. "You were ready to bug out."

Malloy shrugged. "Best laid plans, eh?"

"Where were you? Shuttle docks?" That didn't make sense. The shuttles would be monitored closely prior to the calamity, and the explosions itself had destroyed the launch bay.

He waved his weapon. "Turn around, LC."

Kitchell launched himself through the air and crashed into Malloy.

The two bounced against the wall with a jolt that echoed through the shaft. The flashlight clattered across the floor. Bodies spun and twisted in a mass of arms and legs. Primal grunts echoed through the empty corridor.

The gun went off with a *whumph* and flash of blue light.

Two more shots flared.

The smell of freshly burnt flesh was a razor's edge against the back of Torrance's throat, and Kitchell gave a guttural grunt and then screamed in pain.

Malloy pushed Kitchell's body away, breathing heavily. His expression grew feral. His EVA suit was now grimy and torn. Pools of fresh blood gave zero-g wobbles as it flowed up and around in the middle of the corridor. Malloy waved the gun in Torrance's direction.

Torrance froze.

He couldn't take his eyes off the boy, the horrible way he was gasping for breath, blood flowing from his right side, and his limp arm floating in zero-g. He groaned as he floated away, his eyes wide, his good hand reaching for his wounds.

Torrance moved to go get him, but Malloy leveled the gun at him.

"I hope you're satisfied," Malloy said.

For a moment Torrance thought he would be next.

Instead of shooting him, though, Malloy limped to the explosives and retrieved his flashlight.

"Let's go," he said, motioning down the passage with the gun.

"I need to get Kitchell."

"He's gonna have the same outcome either way."

"I can't leave him like that."

"I said let's go."

Torrance died a little there in *Everguard*'s corridor. He was too far away from Malloy to fight him, and worse, he knew that if he tried and failed there wouldn't be anything left of the ship after Malloy was done.

"Where?"

"I'm in charge now, LC. You just get a move on or I'll blow your goddamned hand off."

Torrance thought of the holo with its ugly black gashes.

Malloy said he was getting off *Everguard*, but Aldrin had reported every docking station was damaged beyond repair.

He glanced at the explosives. Given Central Deck's configuration, a ring of such devices at the outer chamber would result in a cascade of implosions. One place would be safe, though: Pod Engineering.

It made sense.

Pod Engineering was an obvious target during any skirmish, so it had its own vacuum control system to contain potential battle damage. Ironic that a design mechanism meant to save the ship in case the launch room was destroyed might well make that the only part of *Everguard* to survive this attack.

Torrance ran through a list of possibilities before settling on the launch tubes.

"You're going to use a pod to get out," Torrance said. "That's where you were heading before the explosions, weren't you? That's why you ran into me so quickly. It just happened to be close to Systems Command."

"Very bright, Mr. Holmes. Now, are you gonna get going, or am I going to take one of those hands."

Malloy pointed the gun, and Torrance moved.

"What are you planning to do with the engineers controlling the tubes?" he said, thinking about Kitchell and the other two dead men in the hallway. "Just gonna shoot them, too?" Torrance asked.

"I would prefer not to," Malloy said. "But this time it's really up to you."

Chapter 33

UGIS *Everguard*
Ship Local Date: September 15, 2211
Ship Local Time: 1103

Pod Engineering was quiet as they entered the platform overlooking the wide expanse. With backup power engaged, the artificial gravity system was functional. It was under dim lighting, though, and nearly empty. A far cry different from its day of glory.

The pressure of Malloy's gun against Torrance's kidney felt sharp.

The air was as stagnant and thick here as it was everywhere else.

Emergency lighting left dark shadows against the wall like ancient ghosts—he felt them all: images of a countdown, Captain Romanov glancing at him from the corner of his eye, the buzz of confusion when one of the pods turned and flew toward the second planet.

Three men were in the assembly bay now, ostensibly guarding the launch tubes.

The gun ground further into his back.

"Order them away, or I shoot them," Malloy said in a barely audible tone.

Torrance went to the rail. It was cold against his clammy hands.

The engineers looked up, obviously frightened.

Torrance saw the plan now.

Malloy was going to slip into a pod, then autolaunch. Moments later he would detonate the last ring of explosives. Then Torrance and every remaining member of *Everguard*'s crew would be dead. It was how he planned to get away to begin with—why he wasn't in Systems Command when Torrance was making his own last pass.

These engineers might be his only hope, but if he couldn't find a way to send them out of the room, Malloy would shoot them.

Torrance searched the area for something he could use. He thought about automated routines—inventory control and service systems. He considered the electrical conduit. He thought about coded loops that controlled the robotic maintenance and sanitation operations.

An idea tickled the base of his spine.

Malloy pressed the muzzle harder against his kidney.

Torrance spoke to the guards.

"We've got fire on Central Deck Gamma. I need you to join the crew there and wait for orders."

"Captain Yan told us to remain here, sir," one of the men replied.

"Yan's the one who sent me," Torrance lied again. "He needs every able-bodied resource he can get. The all-hands alert would have been broadcast, but communications is down over most of the ship."

"Aye, sir."

"EVA suits and mag boots," Torrance commanded.

The three hustled away.

"Thank you, LC," Malloy said. "I'll sleep so much better now that I didn't have to shoot them. Come, though. No time to waste."

He prodded Torrance down the stairs.

The service panels blinked dim amber. The office upstairs was pitch dark, but it had its own system interface. Would the controllers be active? Would he have to boot up?

Malloy clicked buttons on a handheld device.

The launch tube opened, and an alpha-class probe rolled forward on rails. It was a long unit, fifteen meters, easily. Malloy pressed a code on the pod's panel. The cowling opened to reveal a space barely large enough for him to squeeze into. It had been designed as a service pod, a system that would drop supplies to a camp or colony.

"Incredible," Torrance said when Malloy glanced his way.

"The only way to fly."

Malloy pointed the gun at him again.

"Stand against the wall there, LC. In a moment it will all be over."

Torrance moved away from the pod.

Malloy stepped into the drone and, keeping his weapon trained on Torrance, wedged himself into the pod's cargo slot. "I'm sorry it had to end like this, boss," he finally said.

Torrance fought the urge to glance at the service panel. He gritted his teeth and forced a dry swallow.

"Go on and look at it if you want, LC. Everything's already programmed and running. Even you can't slop code fast enough to change the world today, which makes me glad because I would really, really hate to shoot you."

"You're a true friend, Karl."

Malloy punched another sequence on his handheld, then smiled. "Good-bye, LC."

The lid to the pod closed and the tube began its automated sequence. Its individual airlock activated with a high-pitched whine.

Torrance raced up the stairs and into the dark control room.

He was lucky. The panel was powered—probably necessary for Malloy's plan. He had only as much time as it took the system to purge atmosphere from the tube. After that, the drone would launch, and Malloy would engage the detonator.

His arm ached, and the dim light exposed an ugly bruise that was still growing along the outside of his wrist.

His fingers crawled over the command station as best they could.

He went directly to the service screen.

Maybe it was his imagination, but he could feel the derelict ship respond. *Everguard* was like him in so many ways, slow and out of date, but she responded to him. He hoped she was still ready and able.

Each external service area had its own power backup, so the maintenance robots should be active. The trick would be to get them out of their storage bins and replace their primary cleaning-service command set with a new repair order.

With a few keystrokes he installed the canned routines he had coded to streamline upgrades, and developed the new requirement.

His personal authorization was enough to inject program.

He pressed the command sequence, and the system blinked its answer.

Two square hatches hinged open on *Everguard*'s outer hull. A pair of bullet-headed robots rolled to the edge of the launch tube. Their magnetized bearings and roller skids held them to the surface of the ship until they got to the repair target. They had no way of knowing a drone was inside that launch tube, no way of knowing a man was inside the drone. They also could not have comprehended the fact that the lives of the 453 souls still alive aboard *Everguard* depended upon their actions.

Their programming said the door to tube 1 had to be sealed.

They swapped their utility packages and took positions around the outer edge of the hatch. A few seconds later, they lit their vacuum torches and began the welding procedure. Metal boiled in the localized heat, bonding, then cooling rapidly in the chill of the void.

It would take a few minutes to purge the atmosphere of tube 1.

Pod Engineering grew silent.

Except for one, faint noise. A rattling of breath that came from the corner of the room that he had missed in the panic of the moment.

He turned and saw the dark form of a person lying on the floor, struggling to breathe. As he grew closer, his eyes adjusted.

"Thomas!"

Kitchell's voice was a gurgling whisper. "It's me."

"How ..."

Kitchell bit back a smile. "Who do you think turned on the command panel?"

It became clear. Kitchell had followed them here. He had been unable to catch up, but he snuck in while Malloy was preparing the launch. And he was smart enough to get the system's main computer controller booted up. If he hadn't done that, there wouldn't have been time to activate the bots.

He looked at the kid and nearly cried.

A warning light flashed on the mission control screen.

LAUNCH DOOR LOCK ERROR.

The robots had done their job. The electro-weld was in place, cooling and already strong in the near absolute zero temperature of lunar space.

The autolaunch sequence initiated.

Malloy had been right about one thing.

There was nothing Torrance could do to stop the launch process now.

Torrance took cover behind the panel, hoping the drone's engine wasn't strong enough to break through the weld.

The drone's rocket motor lit with the sound of thunder.

The room shook with a heavy concussion that knocked him off his feet.

When it was over, he stood up, went to the control panel. He keyed in the comm sequence.

"This is Systems Command," a voice he didn't recognize came on.

"This is Lieutenant Commander Black," he said. "I need a bomb squad in Delta Corridor of Central Deck. Now."

"Aye, sir."

They broke connection.

It's over, Torrance thought. It's finally over.

But, of course, it wasn't.

Chapter 34

Aldrin Station
Local Date: December 23, 2214
Station Local Time: 2312

"Are you all right, sir?"

The medic's nametag read *Smythe*. He was maybe thirty, with the thin bone structure that marked him as a lifelong lunar native. His smock was loose and lined with pockets and clips that held meds, instruments, and other such equipment. The shoulder and short sleeve of his left arm were marked with bloody splashes. One knee of his pants was torn.

"I've had better days," Torrance said as he stepped from the shuttle. "But I'm fine."

Smythe sat him down on a gurney and began to examine him.

He had lost track of how long he had been awake now.

Thirty hours?

Thirty-six?

All of them spent on a derelict spacecraft that could implode any moment, and with hundreds or thousands of dead and dying compatriots.

Once *Everguard* had been stabilized, and the hull had been cut through, a shuttle ferried the wounded away. Torrance's damaged wrist had gotten him a ticket here just prior to those who were fully healthy.

The makeshift triage center he stepped into had been constructed in a tube just off Aldrin Station's receiving area. The corridor was a large, rounded connection ring padded with powder-blue mats that had ALDRIN STATION stenciled in haphazard locations. Each section of the tube rotated, creating its own form of centrifugal gravity. The tube itself linked the emergency shuttle locks to the central docking station, where additional processing stations had been set up, and where lift tubes would run the uninjured directly up to Aldrin Station's primary compartments.

Enlisted and officers alike worked to clear the way for stretchers and medical carts. Doctors and nurses huffed it down the corridor, yelling orders and checking readings from instruments attached to their mangled patients.

He saw everything, but his brain wasn't really working.

So mostly he saw blood, skin, and meat that had been charred black. Refuse from sterile bandages littered the area. He saw medical equipment, magnetic-drive gurneys, empty packets of pain meds, and broken utensils.

These were the things that confirmed for him that this whole thing had really happened.

That it had not been merely a never-ending nightmare.

He was on Aldrin, though.

Finally.

For the first time in what seemed like forever no one was looking at him to tell them what to do. It was almost quiet. He was almost alone.

"Holy effin' God," he muttered, flashing on Malloy as he said it.

"Are you all right, Lieutenant Commander?" the medic said.

Torrance scanned the tube behind him.

"Do you have any word on my team?"

"You'll have to be more specific, sir,"

"Lieutenant Marisa Harthing?" he said. "Or Thomas Kitchell?"

He had been asking everyone he saw, but things were confused and no one knew anything concrete. All he knew for sure was that Kitchell was still breathing when he was taken off in the first wave, and that Harthing had not returned directly—and that Rearward Deck had been badly damaged.

"I don't know any specifics," the medic said. "Let me work on that wrist."

Torrance grimaced.

"I've been asking everyone," he said, mostly to himself, mostly just to keep talking. For some reason that seemed important. Keep talking. Keep his brain moving. "No one seems to know anything."

"I hope they're fine," the medic said as he touched Torrance's hand. A spike of pain ran up his arm. The wrist was bruised and swollen. "I think it's broken," the medic said. He placed a pain patch on the back of Torrance's hand, and things got a little better.

"I don't need you to tell me it's probably broken," Torrance said. "What I need is some goddamned help finding out about my team."

"I wish I could do that for you, sir."

The medic gave Torrance a firm stare.

"Do you understand me, sir? I would love to do that, but as you might be able to tell it's kind of a mess around here. When you get through triage you'll get to see Medical Sergeant Boreaux. She should have the full roster, and so she should be able to help you."

Torrance leaned back against the padded wall and gave a defeated nod.

"I'm sorry to be such a pain in the ass," he said as he held out his damaged arm. He wanted to go to sleep.

A voice came out of his dreamy mind.

"Harthing got hit fighting fires on Rearward, sir."

He opened his eyes and looked around, feeling more than a bit strange. The corridor around him lost some focus. Pain meds, probably.

Ensign Whalen sat on a gurney and held a crimson-stained rag to her head. She had gone with Marisa's group.

"It's not as bad as it looks, LC," she said. Her white teeth glowed against her dark skin. "Just a cut."

"Lieutenant Harthing?" he asked.

"She was magic, sir. Got several families out of sealed quarters before she got caught in a collapse. Hope it's not bad, but I can't say anything for sure."

"Thank you," Torrance replied. At least it was something.

Smythe waved a portable X-ray over his wrist.

"It's definitely broken."

"Good call," Torrance replied. His voice sounded distant, but even he could still make out the sarcasm that rode on it.

"I'll get the bone guys over here." He looked at the nametag still pasted to Torrance's uniform and spoke into a communicator. "Abke, I need a nanoknit admin here for Lieutenant Commander Black, Torrance. X87-329. Triage sector green."

"Don't suppose Abke ever gets hurt," he said.

Smythe flashed a grin and holstered the scanner. "No, sir. I don't suppose she does."

The medic wrapped a soft plastic sheath around Torrance's wrist. The wrapping immediately grew rigid and pressed painfully against the back of Torrance's hand, causing him to groan.

"That should do until they get to you. Don't bend it."

"Fat goddamned chance," Torrance said. His hand tingled like he was getting an electric shock, and the intense pain went away. "When can I see the medic you mentioned?"

"Abke, please give Medical Sergeant Boreaux a message that Lieutenant Commander Black would like to see her at her earliest convenience. Use my priority code number two."

He looked at Torrance, then scanned the triage area.

"It might be a while."

"I understand," Torrance said. "Thanks."

Smythe pointed down the hallway.

"Can I get you to stay under the green banner over there so the bone guys know where to find you?"

"Sure."

The medic bustled to the next patient.

Torrance walked to the green banner and took a seat on the floor.

He closed his eyes and leaned back against the soft wall.

Torrance would not want to be in Smythe's shoes. He would lose his mind if he had to deal with this kind of thing every day. Medical folks were either true gifts or bat-shit crazy.

Ensign Whalen's story fit with a few others he had heard: Marisa had made it to Rearward, assessed the situation, and worked to vent several compartments to vacuum in order to block off the spread of fire. But she apparently timed one step incorrectly, or maybe the fire surprised her, and no one had any information on what happened next.

Fire is like that, he thought, as his consciousness faded in and out.

Fire was a perfect microcosm of life.

It grows in places you think it shouldn't be able to, and it can lie in wait while you forget about it, then come back meaner and angrier than ever.

The memory of bodies floating in micro-g made his stomach do flip-flops.

All these people, he thought.

Kitchell. The kid was only twenty-two.

Was he alive?

He thought the rest of his team. He didn't know where they all were, and that made him mad.

And Marisa, of course.

He had ordered Marisa to Rearward, just as he had taken Kitchell into the hallways. The explosion may have killed the rest, but he had ordered these two into danger, and he had given Malloy the lives of three of his crew. He wondered where Yarrow was and what happened to the guy she was trying to save. Ensign Yarrow had been planning to leave the service to be a VP at a construction conglomerate.

The muscles around his neck constricted into a cramp. He used his good hand to rub it down.

Another shuttle arrived from *Everguard* then.

The door to the triage corridor opened, and a column of people stepped into the gate.

"Hey, LC!" a thick voice pulled him from his cloud.

Silvio Nivead walked with a group of crew members.

Torrance waved. "Are you okay?" he said.

"Not a scratch, LC," Silvio said with his plump arms wide out. His smile was like a crescent moon. "I'm glad to see you alive, my friend! You're a hero! A true hero!"

"Sure, I am, Silvio. I'm a real hero."

He smirked and put his head back on the padding.

A moment later, he was asleep.

Aftermath

Chapter 35

Aldrin Station
Local Date: December 26, 2214

The story came out quickly enough. Lieutenant Commander Torrance Black had stopped Malloy, and in doing so, stopped U3 from destroying the rest of *Everguard*. Four hundred and fifty-three people owed their lives to him and his bravery.

The media pool loved it.

Torrance pointed out that without Kitchell, nothing he did would have made a difference, but only a few reporters cared for that kind of nuance and with the war with Universe Three in a new heating cycle, the UG was looking for a hero everyone could relate to right now.

Interstellar Command was not blind to his value.

Torrance was awarded a Presidential Citation for bravery under fire in record time, and a Purple Star for his injury, which meant he got to add a red and gold icon and a purple badge to the mortarboard he wore to each of the funerals he attended over the next two weeks. It also meant that an additional stipend was appended to his paycheck, and that his discharge was placed under review until he could have an interview with Admiral Umaro, the command's top ranking military officer.

It also meant reporters from the pool stuck their microphones in his face everywhere he went, and that the newsfeeds were filled with hatchet jobs that got everything it was possible to get wrong, wrong.

Everyone wanted to know what he thought.

They wanted to hear him call for blood.

"I don't know what to think," Torrance said whenever he could. "I'm just trying to make sense of it all right now."

Chapter 36

Aldrin Station
Local Dates: December 28, 2214

"She was burned over nearly eighty percent of her body."

Torrance was in his quarters, speaking through video projector to the doctor who had finally been made available to brief him. The doctor was in her office, seated behind a desk. The wall behind her held the clichéd images of certifications, diplomas, and other bric-a-brac that Torrance could care less about.

"Can I see her?"

"No." The doctor's face grew lined in the screen. "Nothing personal, Lieutenant Commander, but burn victims need to be isolated to protect them from infection and disease. No one can see her now except the medical staff."

Torrance pressed his lips, unable to make words come.

"She should make it, though. The fact is that we're not really properly staffed or equipped to handle her case here. So we've got a specialist en route from Luna to transport her back there. It's the best medical center in the segment."

"What's going to happen to her?"

"She'll have to grow new skin—which takes time. The base elements will grow rapidly, but full recovery from burns like this can take weeks of therapy to create new nerve endings, and long spans of physical therapy to retrain her nervous system on how to process her new senses. Even then, one hand will probably always be difficult for her to use unless she decides to do a regen procedure."

"I see."

"She's also going to lose some function of her right leg."

They had already told Torrance that the leg had been shattered when a collapsing bulkhead caught her unaware.

He struggled with guilt. He should have sent someone in her place, that's what he thought. But, then, maybe that person wouldn't have built the fire block Marisa had built, and maybe that person wouldn't have saved the lives Marisa had saved. And the truth was that Marisa was true military, and true military runs to trouble, not from it. It was why she had come to Systems Command to begin with. She understood the risks, and she had taken them. She had sacrificed herself to save the rest.

In the end, maybe this was the difference between them.

"And Thomas?" he finally said.

"He's in better shape. Whoever patched him up on the ship saved his life. It'll take a few days for regen to replace his right kidney, and we're doing some work to deal with infection."

"Can I see him?"

The doctor looked almost relieved to say yes.

Aldrin did not include a full hospital, just a basic emergency medical center, so the makeshift hospital ward was a repurposed construct of temporary walls and drapes that had been rolled into an open chamber that was more often used as a dance hall or a conference center. The place had been cobbled together so rapidly that the soft walls were still standing at skewed angles.

A male nurse escorted Torrance through a corridor lit by the domed ceiling lights and a continuous pipe of chemically luminous sticks that ran along the top of wall panels that were thrown together end-to-end. Individual patients' beds were blocked off by cloth screens that made the quality of the lighting vary from segment to segment. The nurse's footsteps were nearly silent, but Torrance's shoes squeaked against the abrasive floor. His hand throbbed as he walked, too. He felt the heat of the bone-bot cells the docs had given him working—mostly along the top of his hand. The sway of his stride made the dull pain well back and forth.

The smell of the makeshift hospital was more neutral than an established medical center, with only a hint of antiseptic here to cover the smell of blood.

A muted whimper came from somewhere.

Someone gave a snorting snore in a nearby compartment.

The nurse whispered as he reached for a corner tab. "He is right here. I think he's asleep."

"That's all right."

The nurse eased the screen back and they slipped through.

Kitchell's form was a shadow lying on the slab of his gurney. Torrance stepped to his side. The smell of plastic skin was thick. The machine recording vitals beat a slow rhythm.

"Can I have a moment?" Torrance finally said.

The nurse appraised him.

"I promise I won't hurt him."

"I'll go check on a few other patients," the nurse said. He pulled back a drape and left them alone.

Torrance listened to Kitchell breathe. Seeing the kid lying in this hospital bed brought him pain that was almost too much to bear.

"Hey, LC," Kitchell said. His voice was thick with sleep or pain meds, but it was solid, the words not slurred.

"Didn't mean to wake you up," Torrance said, but inside he was happy to be able to talk. "How are you?"

"All shot up, I guess."

"I can't believe you jumped a guy who had a gun."

Kitchell tried to shrug, but cringed.

Torrance put his hand on Kitchell's shoulder as the young man caught his breath. The contact made Torrance aware of how cold his hand was. He started to pull back, but then left his fingertips touching.

"I'm sorry I got you shot," Torrance said.

It was the first time he had voiced it, and he realized now that this was the reason he wanted to see Kitchell to begin with. To apologize. To tell him he wished it was the old and washed-up Torrance who was "all shot up," and not the twenty-two-year-old Kitchell. The realization caught in his throat like a dry chicken bone.

"I'll let you jump the asshole with the gun next time," Kitchell replied. "That'll make us even."

Torrance laughed and dabbed at the liquid that was forming in his eye.

"Fair enough," he was finally able to say.

He wanted to ask Kitchell why he had jumped Malloy, but he discovered that he already knew the answer to that question. He had always known it, but he needed to come here and be with Kitchell himself to actually believe it.

"I hope they give you a goddamned medal," Kitchell said.

Torrance gave a sarcastic huff. Kitchell didn't know about the rushed Presidential Citation or the Purple Star. And he didn't know about the Distinguished Medal of Honor Torrance had recommended for Kitchell himself, to hell with whether the kid was official service or not.

"You deserve it, LC. Without you, man ..." Kitchell gasped for a breath, then just sighed and closed his eyes against the pain and the drugs. "None of us make it, you know?"

Torrance wished he had something he could reply with, but he couldn't find a word that was big enough, so he just stood there feeling both jerkish and brilliant, and both smaller and bigger than he ever imagined feeling.

"Do you have the data?" Kitchell said in something that was nearly a whisper.

Torrance put his good hand into his pocket, feeling the sharp edge of the crystal as it pressed into his fingers even after he extracted his hand.

"I've got it."

"That's good."

"Yeah, I know."

"There's something there. I can feel it, man."

The screen rustled.

"We need to leave, Lieutenant Commander."

He swallowed hard and nodded. "All right."

Kitchell reached out and grabbed his good hand. "Don't lose that data, LC. I want to work on it again sometime."

The nurse led him away.

He felt the pressure of Kitchell's grip on his wrist and the memory of the data crystal's hard edge on his fingertips. He thought about the last wormhole pod that might be rusting away on

Eden, and he thought how ironic it was that it would wind up being the last remaining piece of the spaceship he had spent eighteen standards on.

But mostly he thought about a young man who had gotten himself all shot up because it was the only right thing he had to do.

The funerals were a morbid blur.

Kip Levitt was one of them.

The captain's son, Andre Romanov, was another.

In one of those ironic twists of fate that life can throw, Captain Romanov had invited his son to join him on the bridge, otherwise Andre probably would have lived through it all. The captain, though, had been in his briefing room when the explosions came, and that entire chamber had broken from *Everguard* to tumble through space before impacting the lunar surface. Romanov lived, though he lost his forearm and would have to undergo regenerative procedures or wear a prosthetic for the rest of his life.

About the only person Torrance knew who did not receive a funeral with honors was Karl Malloy.

His pod had blown through the launch door on ignition, flattening itself like a hollow-tipped bullet. There hadn't been enough of Malloy left to either hang or bury.

Before the string of funerals, Torrance told himself he was going to pay close attention, that life was going to teach him something as he went through them. But he was wrong. There was nothing there for him—nothing he could put into hard words, anyway. For him, the only thing that came through was that there had been people here one moment—people who had traveled four and a half light years and back at more than half the speed of light, people who had lived and loved and done their jobs, people who had worked together to change the world. Then in one moment they were gone.

That was *all* that happened.

The pall of loss was like looking at the darkest place in space and trying to count the stars, knowing all the while that there was more darkness behind it.

Everything else paled in comparison.

The politics. The anger. The fear.

Nothing else registered with him.

Only the people.

CHAPTER 37

Aldrin Station
Local Dates: January 18, 2215

A memorial was held for the *Everguard* dead, and then the skeleton of the ship was scuttled shortly after.

When the scuttling service had finished, Torrance went to one of Aldrin Station's many observation panels to stand alone and just watch space as it expanded on its way into darkness. It felt as cold and distant as he did. He was tired. He felt stretched in a hundred different ways. He felt out of sync with his quarters in Aldrin Station, and hadn't slept well.

And yet, despite the crevasse of loss that was etched into his mind, he thought about Thomas Kitchell lying in his bed, not giving up, already planning what he was going to do when he was all healed up.

As he looked out at the bright glow of the Alpha Centauri trinary, he pulled the data crystal from his pocket. The Eden files were loaded in that matrix. Its translucent tint made the piece look almost liquid against the palm of his hand.

"LC?"

He put the crystal back into his pocket as he turned.

It was Ensign Whalen, who had also attended the service. She was dressed in a purple sarong draped over a black tank and pants.

"Very nice," Torrance said, motioning the dress. "I haven't seen that before."

"I'm decommissioning, sir. Going Earthside. My parents say some friends, well, they've got a job for me."

"You'll do great."

"I wanted to thank you, sir. For everything you did."

"You're welcome. Let me know if I can ever give you a recommendation."

"Thank you."

They stood and watched space together.

"What are you going to do next, sir?" Whalen asked.

Torrance smiled.

"A few weeks ago I was pretty sure I was going to do the same thing you are."

"And now?"

Kitchell's words echoed in his mind as Torrance turned to her. The boy was still youthful enough to be brash at times, but he was whip smart.

"To be honest with you," he said. "I don't have a clue what's next for me. But a good friend of mine says that when your time comes you have to take a chance. So now I think I'm going to take a little time to get my act together, and then I'm going to do everything I can to find out what life is really about."

Whalen gave a toothy smile.

"Sounds like a wise friend."

"Yes," Torrance said as he stared out into space. "I've learned a lot from him."

This is the end of

STARFLIGHT

STEALING THE SUN: BOOK 1

If you enjoyed this story, you might be interested in the rest of the
series:

STARBURST

STARFALL

STARCLASH

STARBORN

If you enjoyed this story, please consider stopping by your favorite
online booksellers' websites and leaving a review. Word of mouth
is the most powerful force in the universe when it comes to the
livelihood of your favorite authors!

ABOUT THE AUTHOR

Ron Collins is an Amazon best-selling Dark Fantasy author who writes across the spectrum of speculative fiction.

His fantasy series *Saga of the God-Touched Mage* reached #1 on Amazon's bestselling dark fantasy list in the UK and #2 in the US. His short fiction has received a Writers of the Future prize and a CompuServe HOMer Award, and his short story "The White Game" was nominated for the Short Mystery Fiction Society's 2016 Derringer Award.

He has contributed a hundred or so short stories to *Analog*, *Asimov's*, Fiction River Anthology Series, and several other professional magazines and anthologies.

He holds a degree in Mechanical Engineering, and has worked to develop avionics systems, electronics, and information technology before chucking it all to write full-time—which he now does from his home in the shadows of the Santa Catalina Mountains.

Ron's website is: www.typosphere.com
Follow Ron on Twitter: @roncollins13

Sign up for his newsletter to get free stuff!

http://www.typosphere.com/newsletter

ACKNOWLEDGMENTS

As usual, I've got more people to thank than I'll be able to remember. Since, as I noted in the introduction, this work grew out of a story I wrote during a workshop, I'll start by giving posthumous thanks to AJ Budrys. AJ let me know I was onto something with his gruff "pretty good" critique of the original short story, as well as pointers on a few places it could be made better. And I thank Dr. Schmidt for running that story in *Analog* back in the day.

I certainly thank *Analog* readers for giving the short story a runners-up slot in the AnLab Awards voting that year, and to *Locus* for putting it on their Recommended Reading list. Those two things kept me working, even when I wasn't sure how to make it work.

Thanks to my fantastic set of early readers and advance publication group. This kind of support is beyond invaluable in worth, yet impossible to repay. Thank you so much.

Thanks to one of my favorite authors, Robert J. Sawyer, for the very generous comment that somehow made it to the front of the book (sheepish grin).

I also thank every beta reader of the novel in all its stages, of which there have been many—but in particular I want to highlight Sharon Bass for great insight and quite rapid turnaround, and Brigid Collins for putting her finger on the heart of the novel version—which made all the difference to me.

Thanks to my old writers group, the Fishers Five—who waded through early versions of the work when it was…umm…well, you know.

As always, thanks to the most important person in my life—Lisa, whose editing is, of course, brilliant and perfect, and every other superlative you can use here, but whose heart is even better.